Keep My Secrets

A DARK AGE GAP BILLIONAIRE ROMANCE

ANASTASIA
BOOK TWO

KATIE A PEREZ

To the independent brats with a praise kink, but no one to tame them- Daddy Theo is here.
Now do as you're told. Turn the page, and be ready to beg for it.

This book has several open door and explicit sexual scenes, many containing acts of BDSM.

This book is not intended for anyone under the age of 18.

There are also mentions of some heavy topics, including but not limited to:

- Anxiety/Anxiety attacks
- Criminal Activity
- Infidelity (not between MMC and FMC)
- Reference to Drugging (not between MMc and FMC)
- Abuse (verbal from parent)
- Degradation
- Knife play
- Sensation play
- Anal play
- Breath play
- Impact Play
- Bondage
- Discussion of Murder
- Brief reference to suicide
- Brief mention of Erotophonophilia
- Reference to Human Trafficking
- Mentions of Sexual Assault

If any of these things will adversely affect your mental health, please close the book now.

While I did try to take great care in trying to portray the BDSM community accurately, this book is not meant to be used as instructions or a guide

If you are interested in any of the activities you read about between Aria and Theo, please do your own research.

If you need help finding reputable resources to explore further, here are a few resources aimed at education:

- Smut Lovers: The Community
- The Pink Kink Podcast
- The_kinkconsultatnt

https://open.spotify.com/embed/playlist/
32ysfKaZ4zvRxQpvQ1dvkA?utm_source=generator

Outta my Head - Omido, Rick Jansen, Ordell
how could u love somebody like me?- Artemas
Fill The Void(with Lily Rose Depp, Ramsey)- The Weeknd,
Lily Rose Depp, Ramsey
Who Do You Want- Ex Habit
hell of a good time-Haiden Henderson
Scream My Name- Thomas LaRosa
abuse me- Ex Habit
Obsessed-zandos, Limi
Swim- Chase Atlantic
In A Night- Asal
Sleepless- Dutch Melrose
Eyes On You- SWIM
ALWAYS BEEN YOU- Chris Grey
MY EYE$- Toby Mai

CHAPTER

One

ARIA

The door opens gently as Theo enters the bedroom.

"Kneel." His tone demanding, but not angry. I look up from my phone, his eyes meet mine, and my core immediately tightens. His eyes run down my body, reminding me of how he looked at me in the dressing room.

"Everything okay?" I ask, sitting up off the headboard. I didn't expect the conversation to be over so quickly.

"Yeah, nothing that can't wait until morning." He starts unbuttoning his shirt. "Now that you've had some rest, let's finish what we started." He takes a pause before repeating, "Kneel."

I sit up on my knees, waiting for direction. I love the way he takes control. I want to hear him tell me what he wants, how I get to please him.

He steps closer to me, his fingers gently placed under my chin. "Good girl." My breath shakes as I hear his praise.

His thumb lingers under my chin, tilting my face up so I

have no choice but to meet his gaze. The weight of it alone has my body humming with anticipation.

"Stay right there," he murmurs, every word deliberate, controlled.

My breath stutters as he shrugs off the rest of his shirt, tossing it to the ground. I can't keep myself from scanning his body, taking in the tattoos littered across his skin.

Theo leans in, so close that his lips brush the shell of my ear when he speaks. "Do you know what I want from you tonight?"

I press my knees together as lightning shoots through my core from just the way he is speaking to me.

"No." A small smile accompanies the whisper escaping my lips.

A low chuckle rumbles in his chest. He trails his fingers down my chin and down the side of my neck.

"I want to hear the sounds you make when you stop thinking, where all you know is how I make you feel."

My eyes gently close and I lean into his touch.

"Good girl," he whispers, like a promise instead of praise.

Theo's hand grips my throat gently, pulling a startled gasp from my lungs. He gently pushes a piece of hair out of my face.

I let out a soft moan..

"Just like that." He smiles down at me

He leans down, placing his lips just out of reach of mine

.

"Please, Daddy," I whisper.

"Already begging, baby?"

"Yes, Daddy," I plead. His grip tightens around my throat. I want to feel his body on mine anyway I can.

"Are you going to listen?" He pulls back, and I immediately miss the warmth of his breath against my lips. I flex my hand against my thigh, wanting him closer. I nod.

"You're learning," he smiles. "And when you listen," he leans back in, his mouth hovering a breath above mine, "you'll find I'm very generous."

Heat coils low in my belly, my breath begins to quicken. I want his touch.

He smiles before pressing his mouth against mine, claiming me. He kisses me deep. I open, letting him in, letting his tongue explore my mouth.

I reach up to touch him, but the moment my fingers make contact, he pulls away.

"Did I say you can touch?"

"No, Daddy."

"And what happens if you can't keep your hands to yourself?"

"You take them away." He leans in, kissing me again.

"You're such a good listener." He leans me back, laying me against the bed.

He cages me in, placing his hand on either side of me.

He lets out a low growl, rough against my throat. "Mine."

"Yours," I whisper. Theo smiles down at me before starting to lift my shirt up my body.

Arching my back, I help him. I want to feel his skin against mine in any way I can get it. He lifts to his knees and unbuckles his belt. Sliding it from his belt loops, my core tightens at the sound of the belt snapping against itself.

He smiles as he stands from the bed and slides his pants down his legs, kicking them off in the direction of his shirt. His eyes watch me as if I am prey.

"On your stomach," he commands, and I do as I am told. Moments later, his hands are on the waist band of my underwear, gently sliding them down my legs. I am now fully exposed to this man, and just the thought has wetness pooling between my legs. Kneeling behind me, Theo lifts my hips, bringing me to my knees. My hands grip the sheets, a soft whimper escaping my lips. I need him. I need his touch. I need to feel him inside me. Whatever Theo wants, I will give if I can feel his cock inside me as I cum.

"So needy." Theo's voice vibrates through my entire body before he slides his dick inside me. I tighten around him, adjusting to his size.

"Fuck," I breathe out. This is exactly what I wanted. He slowly pulls himself out to where only his tip is inside me. I push my hips back, wanting more of him again. He just laughs before slamming back into me.

He repeats this multiple times, knowing what he is doing to me. I look over my shoulder and Theo is smiling down at me. He likes watching me beg. He likes seeing me on the verge of release and not giving me that out.

"Please, Daddy," I beg.

"Not yet," is his only response.

Heat spreads under my skin, my core tightens, my breath hitches, and before I can fully fall over the edge, he pulls me back.

We continue this game for what feels like hours. He always lets me get close, but never lets me finish.

At the end my body is trembling, and I can barely form words.

"Please," my broken whispers plead.

"Good girls get to cum, baby." He thrusts gently. "Brats need to earn it." He thrusts harder, proving his point. I pushed him in the dressing room. I purposely withheld what he wanted. I wanted this.

"Daddy," I begin to plead. I don't know how much longer I can handle this.

"Give me a color," he says, holding himself inside me. I can feel his dick twitch and my body clenches around him. "I need a color, Aria."

"Green," I breathe. This may be torture, but it is delicious torture. I know when he finally allows me to cum it is going to be the most intense orgasm I have ever had, and I need it.

He slams into me harder, pushing himself as deep inside me as he can go. My arms are barely able to hold my body up,

One of his hands stays on my hip, not letting me pull away, the other wraps around my body. His fingers find my clit, and even the slow, gentle motion has pressure building everywhere.

"Have we learned our lesson?" Theo asks.

"Ye-Yes, Daddy," I answer before continuing to beg. "Please."

"Are you going to listen?"

"Yes."

"Good girl," he says as he begins to move his fingers faster. The pressure in my body is about to burst. I almost feel like he is going to pull away as I get close again, but he doesn't. I buck my hips as he circles my clit. My core spasms as I am finally able to feel the release. I cry out as everything finally boils over.

"Such beautiful noises, baby girl," Theo whispers before thrusting a few more times. On the last thrust, he pulls out and releases all over my back.

"What a beautiful mess we make." He flips me over, resting his body on top of mine. I was right. My core still tightens and spasms around nothing. He is no longer inside me or touching me in a way that would elicit this response, but somehow my climax is lingering.

I wrap my arms around his neck, not wanting him to leave. He brushes hair out of my face before kissing the top of my head.

"Let's get you cleaned up so you can get some rest," he says so softly. I nod my head. He gently picks me up and carries me to the bathroom.

CHAPTER
Two

ARIA

I don't know what I was expecting Theo's apartment to look like, but this wasn't it; yet somehow it is so incredibly him. Maybe I was expecting everything to be cold, almost sterile, like walking through a museum and being scared to breathe too hard in a particular direction. Surprisingly, even with the cool tones and metal accents, it's fairly cozy.

"So if you were serious about wanting to move in, this is yours now. Do whatever you want to make yourself feel comfortable." Theo's voice pulls my attention away from the wall of windows overlooking the city.

"It's perfect." A soft laugh escapes my lips with the words. "Unexpected, but perfect." Theo's body suddenly presses against mine, the heat from his chest has me remembering how our bodies were entangled less than an hour ago. It still baffles me how he can go from strong and intimidating to someone who makes me so comfortable, effortlessly. He smiles as my body relaxes into his. As we walk around yet another floor of his penthouse, I am not sure why someone living alone needs this much space, but I guess when you have money to burn, you might as well spend it.

I try to find any personal effects, pictures, or trinkets that would give me more insight into who I am now living with. As I look around, everything seems to be specifically curated and not family items that would have been passed down. Maybe he has the sentimental items somewhere away from where guests might find them, especially since people he works with just show up unannounced at 1:00 a.m. Is that just a social norm for the 1%?

"Do your bosses show up randomly a lot?" I ask as he leads me quietly down the hall.

"Not usually, but due to the nature of our business, there will be times I am given little to no notice, like tonight." When Theo talks about work, his entire body shifts, it's almost like he is two completely different versions of himself; the one who does whatever he does for the association, and the one he is with me.

"Why were they here?" I try not to be pushy about it. He didn't answer when I asked before, but I think that is because he was just wanting to fuck again. Maybe asking now, I'll get a more accurate answer.

"They need me on a work trip last minute." I wait for him to elaborate, but he doesn't.

"When?" I am assuming pretty soon, or they could have waited until Monday to tell him. I press my body closer to his, I am becoming addicted to the feeling of his presence. Not just the adrenaline and dopamine high from sleeping with him, but even the calm that being near him brings over my body.

"Tomorrow, but it won't be for too long," he says before kissing my hand. "You'll have the place to yourself tomorrow night." Before Theo, if I had been told I would have a luxury penthouse to myself for a night, I would have been so excited that I would immediately start planning a huge party. Right now, I am just focused on the spot in my chest that is currently full from the care and adoration from Theo, knowing it will feel hollow tomorrow.

Theo begins to walk us out of the hall and back into the living area.

"What are they needing you to do?"

"Consult on a project some of the younger associates have proposed." He is technically answering my questions, but being vague enough that I'm still not given any actual information. Maybe it's because all I knew growing up was secrets, that knowing he is keeping things from me doesn't sit well, but I also can't be too pushy. We literally met a few days ago, and with no long term commitments, he doesn't have to tell me anything.

"The rest of the items we purchased from the store will be delivered tomorrow. If you need anything else, feel free to get it."

"With what money?" I laugh as he pulls me down on the couch next to him, "My savings are dwindling, and I need to use it to pay off my student loans. Acadia wasn't cheap." I laugh. I really need to start looking for a job. I'm sure there are plenty of architecture firms out here. Even if I can't find something right away, I'm sure I'll be able to find something eventually.

Theo stands and walks to the kitchen, and grabs something off the counter before returning.

He pulls something out before tossing the leather wallet back down. He walks over and begins to hand me a small piece of metal before pulling it just out of reach. I sigh and give him my best puppy dog eyes.

"I will hand this over to you, but I have some conditions." I look up at him, waiting for more information. "I want to know what you're buying. I don't care what you spend, but I do want you to show me the things you are purchasing." I nod my head, it's a reasonable request. "Also while I am gone, if you leave the house I want to know. When you are not home, I want hourly updates unless specified otherwise." I nod again. He lowers the card down slightly to where if I stretched the slightest bit further I could grab it. "And finally, I want you home by nine every night unless you have been given explicit permission, and I want proof of life on that camera right there." My eyes follow as he points to the security camera that has a view of the living room all the way back to the front entry way.

The weight of the card surprises me when he puts it in my hand.

"What is this?" I ask before turning it over and seeing a centurion engraved on the front.

"My Amex, buy whatever you need. Honestly, just get whatever you want."

"You're kidding me." I look down at one of the most coveted pieces of titanium in awe. When I look back up to Theo, he is already looking at his phone, like he didn't just hand me access to his entire bank account. "So I could go spend $100,000, and you would just be ok with that?"

"I told you I want to provide for you, I want to give you the best of everything. While I am away, get the things that will make this feel more like your home. Get the things you need to start over. We can still have movers go get your things, but there is no reason you should go without when I am more than capable of giving you everything you need."

"That you are," I mumble. From life-altering orgasms to a fucking Amex, Theo has not held back on giving me anything, but I can't shake the *it's too good to be true* voice living in the back of my brain. Theo must see the second-guessing, because he immediately grabs my chin and brings my gaze to his. His eyes flick back and forth between mine, making sure I'm paying attention before he says, "When I told you I wanted to give you a fresh start, I meant it. You did not deserve to be treated the way you were growing up, and I want to make sure you have everything you need to take full advantage of this second chance."

Before I can think better of it, the words tumble out of my mouth, "But what's the catch?" I can see a brief hint of hurt in Theo's eyes, and my chest aches. I immediately try to apologize, "I'm sorry, I didn't mean to—"

Fuck. Here he is trying to help me, and I all but accuse him of trying to buy sex.

"Baby, I don't want you to think I am in any way trying to manipulate you or take advantage of you." He leans down and brushes a piece of hair behind my ear. "This isn't a conditional offer. Even though I love how you submit to me in the bedroom and give me control over your body, even if that all stops right now, I still want to provide this for you."

I nod my head softly. He kisses my forehead before walking back to his spot on the couch. He taps his screen a few more times before putting his phone face down on the arm of the couch.

"Don't worry about your student loans, they have been taken care of. Now start thinking about the things you are going to need."

"Yes, Daddy," I say playfully as I quickly add his Amex to my Apple Wallet. I can see the smile on his face out of the corner of my eye. He really likes it when I call him that. It has never been one of those pet names I gravitated towards, but with Theo, not only does it make him really happy, it just feels right.

"So this Daddy thing..." I pause, trying to find the right way to ask without making him think I don't like it. "Is it just a bedroom thing or do you like it all the time?"

"I like hearing you call me Daddy all of the time, in every type of scenario, but I'm not going to push anything you're not comfortable with."

"No, I like it. It feels right." My lips lift into a smile as I can see the slightest sigh of relief in Theo's shoulders. "I do have a question, though." He focuses his gaze on me and waits for me to continue. "What does this kind of relationship look like? Like, I understand the sex part. I love the sex part, but what does it look like during all the other parts? What is this even called? I mean, other than Daddy issues?" I can't help but laugh, but it's true. Most of the time, when women call their partners Daddy, it's assumed it's because they have Daddy issues and are seeking that type of pseudo relationship. I have Daddy issues, but not in that way, I don't think.

"Are you trying to put a label on us, or asking in general?" he clarifies.

"I'm not sure, both?" It's the honest answer. I want to know where the line is. Do I get to ask questions and know about Theo's life, or is this a sugar daddy situation where we fuck and he spoils me, but that's as deep as it goes? Where do I stand?

He takes a moment before speaking, as if he is trying to make sure he is using the right words.

"So, usually a dynamic like ours would be considered Dom/Sub. Where one person is more dominant and takes a leading role in the relationship and activities. I would be considered a Daddy Dom. I would be the provider, and I like to be able to take control, so all you would have to worry about is enjoying your time with me." That dynamic sounds nice. I could really get used to it, but the fear of becoming dependent on him and him being able to withdraw provisions, leaving me with nothing, is like a rock in my stomach.

"For some, the dynamic is only sexual, for others it is a 24/7 lifestyle. There are even some where there is no sex involved. It is really up to the people participating."

"And which are we?"

"That's something we need to decide. The way we have been with each other over the last few days has given me a taste of what living a 24/7 lifestyle would be like with you, and to be honest, I loved it. I loved you blindly trusting me, I loved watching you do exactly as you were told, letting me take control. I loved being in a position to provide for and protect you. But it's not only about me."

I nod, remembering what it felt like to relinquish all control and let Theo take over, not just during sex, but when he was taking care of me and making sure I was fed, or that I was ok after being roofied, or even after being told my mom was a whore. Maybe that is part of why I've been so attracted to him, because he truly cares about me.

"So I would have to listen to everything you say?"

"The things we agreed upon, yes. If there are things you are not comfortable giving over control of, that's fine. We just need to discuss it so we are on the same page."

"And if I don't listen to you, what happens?" Heat settles in my stomach as the different scenarios playout in my head.

"If you disobey, there will be punishments. Again, all agreed upon beforehand, but if you decide to push the boundaries, there will be consequences. Some I'm sure you think you would enjoy, others you..." he pauses as the corners of his lips lift into a knowing smirk, "won't."

Is he thinking about the things he would do to me? Is he imagining the punishments he will give me right now? The thought has me tightening around nothing, remembering the *consequences* I got in the dressing room.

"Ok."

"Ok, what?" He smiles slowly. He needs me to say it. There needs to be no gray; this is black or white. I'm in or I'm out.

"Ok. I will give you control inside and outside of the bedroom. I want you to be in charge." His smile widens as his hands grip my face and pull me into a kiss. This kiss is different; it's not full of lust like the ones before. It's almost as if he's thanking me. For giving him control? For liking what he likes? For just existing?

I smile against his lips as he begins to pull away. He relaxes back into the corner of the couch and pulls me into him.

"We will go more in depth when I get home about rules and boundaries for both of us, so while I am gone I need you to be thinking about your hard limits." I pull my phone out and begin browsing my shopping lists to see what I want to buy with Theo's money. If spoiling me makes him happy, who am I to say no? He tilts my phone down when I don't answer.

"Aria." I smile, and look over my shoulder at him. "Did you hear me?"

"Yes, Daddy." I smile, he presses his lips to my neck.

"You're going to be so much trouble aren't you?" I let out a breathy moan as he grazes his teeth over my neck. "Keep shopping," he instructs.

I lift my phone up and do as I am told. I scroll past a drafting desk and pause. I want it, but I also don't need it right now. I don't even have a job lined up or a place to put it. I start to scroll away when Theo stops me.

"Why didn't you get it?" he asks.

"I don't even have a job or any idea when I'll get one. Plus, where would I put it? All your rooms are full of furniture." It's not like on night one I can insist on him throwing away a room full of furniture so I can have an office for a non-existent job.

"You have an interview on Monday, so you'll need it soon. And tell me which room you want and it's yours."

"You can't be serious."

"Which part?"

"Both?"

"You have an interview on Monday with Castin Construction. It's for a receptionist position, but it's at least a foot in the door, getting you closer to where you want to be." He sounds so assuring, like he really believes I can just walk in and get a job at one of the top architectural firms in the state.

"Why?"

"Why what?"

"Why did you get me an interview? Don't you want me to fully rely on you and let you provide?" Isn't that the Daddy part he was talking about, wanting to be the one providing for all my needs?

"Yes, eventually. But I know there is no way in hell you are going to trust me overnight. I want you to take all the time you need to build trust between us, and if having a job and your own income gives you some peace of mind while you do that, then that's what we need to do." He is still providing for me, just in a different way. He is giving me the space to become comfortable with letting him take care of me. Maybe this can be real.

"The loft." Theo tilts his head back to look at the metal railing above us that circles an open loft.

"Done, it's yours. We will have someone come clear out the furniture when I get home from the trip."

I smile as I settle against his chest and begin scrolling for new furniture.

CHAPTER
Three

ARIA

"Hey, Baby," Theo whispers.

"Mmmhhmmm," is all I reply while I try and roll over so the sun is not in my face.

"I'm leaving, so I need you to sit up." His tone is still gentle, but he is giving me instructions to follow. I momentarily contemplate not listening, but I have a better idea. I sit up, pulling my pillow against my body and resting my head on the top. He said I had to sit up, not that I had to wake up.

"Aria," he scolds.

"Daddy," I scold back. I can hear the quiet laugh he is trying to suppress. I slowly open one of my eyes and peek at him over my pillow. He is looking down at me with an amused smile.

"Hey, I am getting ready to leave and need to talk to you before I go." I let out an over dramatic sigh before lifting my head off the pillow and look at him.

"I should only be gone a night or two. If you need anything, I put Mia's number in your phone, and Enzo is downstairs and can get you anything you need." He pauses, taking me in. "Do you remember the rules I laid out yesterday?" He rolls his sleeves up over his forearms, and I can't help but watch. I never understood the stereotype of women finding forearms sexy, but watching Theo definitely has my heart racing.

"Uhmm, home by nine, proof of life, and send you screenshots of how I'm spending your money," I rattle off.

"And?" he asks, encouraging me to remember.

"And?" I ask back, because I woke up literally thirty seconds ago and barely know my name.

"If you leave the house, I want to know and to receive hourly updates."

"See, I didn't remember that because I don't plan on leaving the house." I smile up at him, proud of my excuse. It is true, I wasn't planning on going anywhere. Today was going to be a sleep and shop kind of day. Two things I love to do in bed, amongst other things.

"And because you forgot a rule, I'm going to add one."

"How's that fair? If I can't remember five, how am I supposed to remember six?" I roll my eyes. He leans down, putting his arms on either side of me, caging me in.

"No orgasms without my permission." My eyes shoot open as I make contact with his.

"You're a masochist," I whisper. He leans in and presses his lips against mine.

"Sadist, baby. The word you're looking for is *sadist*." He kisses me again. "And this is just the tip."

"I like your tip," I breathe against his lips.

"Oh, I know you do." He smiles again before kissing me deeper, and wrapping one arm behind my back, pulling me in. It's just a kiss, but it has butterflies swarming in my stomach.

"Last time, what are the rules?" He pulls away just enough that I can't kiss him, and puts his arm back on the bed beside me.

"Tell you if I leave the house, hourly updates, home by nine, proof of life, tell you how I'm spending your money, and no orgasms without permission." I grit that last rule out between my teeth.

"Good girl." I smile at the adoration. "Again, this trip shouldn't take too long, so I'll be home soon. But if I am not, good luck with your interview. You're going to do great." He kisses my forehead. "And remember, good girls get rewarded, and broken rules have consequences." That sentence ties knots in my stomach. The kind that are somehow both uncomfortable yet still pleasant.

I just nod, hoping for one more kiss. Moments later, he gently places one of his hands on the side of my face and leans down for one of the most gentle kisses he has ever given me. I can't help but smile like a giddy child. He steps back, grabs his suitcase, and begins to leave the room.

"Daddy," I call out before he is gone. He turns and looks at me. "You said, you don't care how much I spend?" He nods. "But really, what's the budget?"

He lets out an amused laugh before smiling and saying, "I guess you will just have to spend to find out."

I roll my eyes and let my body flop back onto the bed. *No limit?* There has to be a limit. I guess I will start shopping and see where he draws the line.

I pull my phone off the charger and begin scrolling. I have an interview to prepare for, and I don't know if I purchased anything interview-worthy the other night. Let's start with the fun part, shoes.

I quickly look up Louboutins. I have no idea what my pay will be at this place if I even get the job. This may be my only chance to get the shoes of my dreams. The thought of buying them online doesn't sit right with me. I want to go to the store and be catered to while picking out a pair—or several.

> Hi, Mia, it's Aria. Theo said I could call you if I needed anything.

Of course, what do you need?

> Would you want to go shopping with me?

CHAPTER
Four

ARIA

I shouldn't have asked her to spend the day with me. This is probably really awkward for her. Before I have the chance to text her not to come, there's a knock on the door as it slowly opens. Of course, she has a key.

"Aria? It's Mia."

"Hey, come on in, I'm almost ready," I shout from the bedroom. Trying to calm my nerves, I take a deep breath and stand up off the bed. "Just grabbing my shoes."

"Take your time. Have you eaten yet?" she asks as I hear her keys hit the counter. I walk out into the living room and feel like I've walked into a wall.

Mia is not what I was expecting. I guess it is kind of a cliché—rich CEO with a hot assistant. Part of me wants to get jealous, ask if they ever had a thing, but the other part knows I'm temporary, and I'm probably just another girl he's brought home.

How many other girls has he had Mia help with? How

many times has she gone shopping with Theo's flavor of the week?

"Oh, you're cute." She smiles before she says, "Shit, sorry that was inappropriate." She blushes, but I smile back. I like her. She's probably not much older than me, with long, dark hair curled to perfection. She looks like she belongs in the city.

"I take it Theo doesn't usually have the best taste in women?" The second the sentence is out of my mouth, I regret it. I don't want to know.

"Wouldn't know. He's never brought anyone home before." That gets my attention. What does that even mean?

"Never?"

"Not to my knowledge. I know he's been in what he considers *relationships* before, but he's never brought anyone home. He's really protective of his space." Yet here I am, alone in his penthouse, waiting on a furniture delivery to create my own space. My gaze looks up toward the loft, wondering what it all means.

"What do you mean by *'what he considers relationships'*?" Does she know that he likes a certain dynamic? Was she ever in that kind of relationship with him?

"What we would consider a situationship, he views as a type of relationship. But he never brings them here. They never go out on dates just because. I don't try to pry into his personal life. But being around him so often, I get the sense they are just hook ups, but he feels bad for calling them just hook ups." Her phone buzzes and it pulls her attention away. Her demeanor turns serious for a brief moment, but relaxes before returning her gaze to mine. Remind me to play poker with her, she is such an easy read.

"Everything ok?"

"Yup, just some work stuff."

"If you're busy today, you don't have to come out with me." Day one in Theo's life and I'm already inconveniencing those around me.

"Nope, I told them I was out of office on a project for Mr. Reeves. You really think I would give up a day of shopping to sit in an office and listen to old men talk? No thanks."

I can't help but laugh. If this situation wasn't so weird, I could see us being close friends. Maybe we still can be, I mean she doesn't work for me.

"Where are we going?"

"Well, I have an interview on Monday and need some office attire, and I need a new laptop. And then we can really go and do anything we want." I flash Theo's Amex, and I can see the wheels turning behind Mia's eyes. This is going to be so fun.

My phone buzzes, and I look down to see Theo's name flash across the screen.

"Hello?"

"Hey, Baby, everything ok?"

"Yeah, why? What's up?"

"I saw Mia had come over. Wanted to make sure nothing was wrong."

"Watching the cameras?" I laugh. I'm not even surprised.

"I got a notification that someone had entered the house, wanted to make sure you were safe," he explains.

"Thank you for being concerned. But no, nothing is wrong. I asked her to take me shopping today to get the things I need for my interview. I hope that's ok."

"Sounds good. Be safe, and hourly updates."

"Will do. Now that I'm going shopping and spending your money, do you want to give me a budget?"

"I've told you before, no budget. Buy what you need, get whatever you want. The card won't decline." I can't help but roll my eyes, but if he says to spend, I'll spend.

"We're about to take off. I expect proof of purchases and location updates when I land."

"Yes, Daddy," I say before remembering Mia is standing in the room, but I can hear his smile when he responds.

"Good girl. I'll see you soon."

The call ends, and I look over towards Mia, who is not hiding the fact that she really wants to address the Daddy comment.

"Ready?" is the only word she utters, even though I can see the gears turning behind her eyes.

"Yup, let's go."

EIGHT HOURS LATER, over half a million spent, I now have an entire closet full of office-appropriate clothing, four new pairs of red-bottomed heels, a new MacBook, iPad, Apple Watch, a snake skin Birkin bag, and several things I bought with the intent of getting a reaction from Theo. But even when I sent him the receipt for Prada paperclips, he just said something about needing good-quality office supplies.

On our way to the restaurant Mia had gotten us reservations for, I sent a selfie with a location update and decided to tally up how much we spent today.

$648,732.

I'm looking down at the calculator on my phone when Theo's name takes over the screen.

"Hi," I say nervously.

"Baby, what's wrong?"

"Uhmm. I wish you had given me a limit."

"Why?" His voice is somehow both concerned and amused. I understand the concern. I just spent more than most people make in a decade in eight hours. I know he told me to find the limit, and he would have stopped me if I was going too far, but what if he was busy and wasn't seeing the updates, and now I've crossed the line?

"We spent $648,700 today." I brace myself for him to get upset.

"$650,000? That's it?" *That's it. That's it? What does he mean, that's it?* That's life-changing money, and he is acting like it's spare change. I look at Mia, who is definitely enjoying watching this conversation. She would have told me if I was spending too much, wouldn't she? Or was she hoping I'd spend way too much and Theo would get mad and end things? No, she wouldn't. She has been nothing but friendly and supportive all day; she knows more about Theo's finances than I do. She would have stepped in if I were putting her boss in a bad spot financially; her job depends on it.

"So that's ok?"

"Do you like the things you got?"

"Yes."

"Then yes, you're absolutely fine. Go spend more if you want. Have fun. Do not worry about the finances, baby, that's my job." My body relaxes into the seat. Moments after hanging up, the car stops in front of the restaurant, and Mia looks over to me.

"How you got one of the most emotionally unavailable, yet seriously powerful men in the city to become obsessed in less than a week needs to be studied. Over dinner, you need to tell me your secrets. Working for Mr. Reeves is great and all, but I'd love for a man to hand me his Amex and say *Go wild*. Girl, you are living my dream." We laugh as we exit the car.

Over dinner, I find out that Mia is twenty-six and has a degree in business from Acadia. We bonded over college anecdotes, and it was fun getting to reminisce even though we weren't there at the same time. She has a pet cat named Daphne and has a small circle of friends in the city. Apparently, even being one degree away from power is close enough for people to try and abuse your position. Noted.

I look down at my phone and note that it's 7:30. If I want to make it home in time for Theo's check-in, we need to be leaving soon.

"Let's get the check and then I need to head home." Mia checks her phone, noting the time.

"Sounds good, let's not get you in any trouble." She smiles. *Does she know?* It doesn't matter either way; all that matters is that I've made a friend, and I don't want to piss off Theo on night one.

CHAPTER
Five

ARIA

Enzo has a few of the concierge staff help me carry all my bags upstairs. It's a type of surreal watching bags with luxury brands plastered on the side parade through my front door. Not to mention I'm gripping my new Birken like my life depends on it. Enzo had offered to bring it up for me, but when my new bag costs more than a house, I am not trusting anyone with it. I may need to sell it in a couple of months; it needs to stay pristine.

Finally, everyone leaves and I'm left alone, surrounded by boxes of clothes and shoes and paper clips. I was told to make myself at home, so I'd better find a place to put all my stuff.

Walking into Theo's bedroom, I can see that he has space in his closet for all my new things, but a knot forms in my stomach at the thought of putting my stuff with his. It feels too much, too fast. He has said this is my home, too, but he is protective of his space. Taking over part of his closet seems like I'm taking things too far.

I close the door and walk into one of the guest rooms. There is minimal decor, a large bed with a metal bedframe, a dresser, and a nightstand. I can make this my room. I can definitely add some things that make it feel more me, like a rug and a lamp. I can get some art for the walls and maybe a new duvet cover.

Done. This is my new room. When Theo comes home, if he wants me to sleep in his room, I can do that, but this room will be my space.

I start bringing all the bags into the room and lining them up on the floor, and throwing some on the bed.

Pulling all my clothes out of the boxes, I lay them on the bed so I can grab some hangers and put them away.

I open the closet door, hoping to find some, but hangers become way less important when I realize what is in this closet.

Laid out on the closet shelves are sex toys.

Lots of them.

Hanging on one of the walls are paddles and lots of leather. I'm not sure what a lot of these are, but I know what they are used for.

I walk further into the closet, and there are several shelves with neatly bound rope, cuffs, and even nipple clamps.

I pick up one that has four screws. Twisting one set and watching it tighten sends lightning to my core.

These are Theo's. He has all this because it's what he likes. He is going to want to use these on me. A brief moment of panic has me holding my breath, but even with the slight fear, my body fills with desire. Just thinking about Theo handcuffing me to the bed and using some of these on me has my nipples hard.

I run my fingers along the strips of leather that are attached to a handle, wetness pooling in my underwear.

I look back over to the shelf of vibrators, trying to decide which one to use to help relieve the pressure that built up in my core. Before I can grab one, my phone rings.

Shit! What time is it?

I rush out to my phone.

"Daddy. I'm sorry I—" I say, trying not to sound out of breath.

"Where are you?"

CHAPTER
Six

THEO

The living room is empty. It's 9:05 and I've been staring at this security camera feed, and the living room is still empty.

Her location says she should be home, and I saw her enter the penthouse, but also saw several men follow, and I haven't seen her since they left. I give her a few more minutes before I call.

Garret and Eddie are talking logistics. How many targets, and how many Knights we would need.

"I need to make a call. Can we come back to this in a few?" My words are short. I need to go find out where Aria is and why she's not where she's supposed to be.

Garret looks at his watch before looking at Tatum.

"We should break for dinner, anyway. Meet back here at eleven?"

Eddie nods before looking back at me, trying to figure out why I am about to walk out of a planning session. We normally work through the night and eat or sleep when we're done.

Once everyone has agreed to break, I walk out of the room and immediately hit call.

Eddie is a step behind me, trying to keep pace.

"What is going—" he starts asking, but Aria picks up.

"Daddy, I'm sorry I—"

"Where are you?" I growl into the phone.

I look over my shoulder to Eddie mouthing *Daddy?* I guess he can hear Aria, even if she is not on speaker.

"Aria, answer the question," I demand, and I can see the dots connect for Eddie. He smiles before mouthing *Daddy* with a mischievous smile as he leans against the wall, arms crossed. I don't have time to bother with him right now. I'll deal with that situation later. Right now, my focus is on Aria.

Where is she? Is she ok? Did she forget? Did someone hurt her?

"I'm home, I promise. I just..." she pauses. "I just got distracted. I'm sorry."

"Distracted with what? Where are you?" I hate having to ask again.

"I'm in a guest room..." she says softly, like she's scared to tell me. Why would she be scared to tell me she's in one of the empty bedrooms?

Then I remember what is in the room next to my bedroom. Fuck. I was planning on showing her, but I wanted to be there when she found it.

I hit the FaceTime button and wait for her face to show on the screen. She's looking at the floor. She really thinks I'm going to be angry that she is in there.

"Baby." I try to stay calm. "Look at me."

She slowly brings her gaze back to the screen. I can tell she's looking at her phone, but not looking at me.

"I'm sorry," she whispers.

"Why? What are you apologizing for?" She did nothing wrong. I gave her a few rules, and the only one she broke was not being in the living room at nine.

"I shouldn't be in here, I shouldn't have touched your things."

"Hey, what were my rules?" I need to remind her of what we agreed. I told her to make herself at home, and that's exactly what she did.

"Tell you if I left, hourly updates, tell you what I was buying, home by nine, proof of life, and no orgasms," she recites. She isn't registering the words, just rattling off the rules.

"And in any of those did I say you can't go in there?" I ask, hoping this makes it clearer.

"No?" she asks. That's progress.

"Did I say you can't touch?"

"No." Her voice sounding more confident. She's getting it.

"Did you get off?" Her cheeks flush red.

"Not yet." So she likes what she sees. She was planning on getting herself off to the idea of me using some of those things on her. My cock twitches at the thought.

"Then the only rule broken is that you weren't in the living room for proof of life." She did break a rule, but we can deal with that later.

"I'm sorry." Her voice soft again, but not as scared.

I walk into my room and close the door behind me.

"I was planning on showing you that stuff when I got

home, but since you found it already. Do you have any questions?"

The gears are turning in her head. She has questions, she just doesn't know what to ask.

After a minute of silence, she asks, "Do you like to use these things on others, or have others use them on you?"

I smile. "I like to use them on others."

"So you like to cause pain." That was more of a statement.

"I know that's how it can be perceived, but I don't necessarily get off on inflicting pain. I enjoy being able to provide a safe place for someone to explore their more *unconventional desires*." Being the one able to provide feelings and sensations that one craves, but is told are wrong, is a level of trust that cannot be compared. "Pain being one of them."

"How? How do you know what to do?" she asks.

"We talk about it. You tell me what your hard limits are, what you want to explore, and I tell you different things I enjoy. There will always be a discussion of what is ok and what isn't."

She sits on the bed.

Yes, Aria, get comfortable. We have a lot to discuss.

She takes a deep breath.

"You seem nervous." She looks away again. "What's going on?"

"I don't know."

"Aria."

"I don't know," she repeats. "I have questions, but I don't know what the questions are," she admits, her voice soft.

"Then what if I ask some questions?"

"Ok."

"Will you answer honestly?"

"Yes, Daddy." This is not an easy conversation. I am asking her to be vulnerable with me, and I am not even in the same room.

"When you think about the toys you saw...Do they scare you? Or do they make you curious?" I ask, starting off easily.

"Curious," her voice soft.

"Good."

Aria rolled onto her side. "And what if I said some of them did scare me?"

"Then I'd say you're honest," I reply. "Fear isn't weakness, Aria. It's information. And it tells me where to go slow, and where to..." I swallow, "push."

"Push?"

"Yes, I want to be able to give you the experiences you want, to feel those sensations you have only been able to fantasize about. That would require me to be gentle in some areas, and not so much in others. I can push some of your boundaries and help you find release in ways you have only dreamed of. Toys are just tools. The real question is whether you trust me enough to use them ways you need, not ways you fear."

Aria closes her eyes. She is taking in everything I have to say.

"And if I say yes?"

"If you said yes, I would get to spend a lot of time proving that surrendering to me isn't giving up control, it's finally being free of it."

Her breath trembles, and for a moment, neither of us speaks. I can see the battle in her eyes. She has been told certain desires are wrong, and now she is hearing that I want to help her feel everything.

"Say the word, Aria. Let me show you."

She nods.

"Say it."

"Yes, Daddy."

"Put the phone on the nightstand where I can still see you." She does as she's told. "Close your eyes for me."

She does without hesitation. I want the room around her to fade into darkness, to solely focus on my voice.

"Good girl," I praise. "Now, imagine I'm there with you. Imagine me going into the closet where I keep everything you found. Which toy do you think I'd choose first?"

"I-I don't know," she stutters.

"Yes, you do," I counter, my voice steady. "Your body already gave you the answer the moment you saw it."

Her breath quickens. "The cuffs."

"Mmm." *She already knows.* "You look perfect with your hands bound. No distractions, just me and my touch."

Aria shifts; she likes what she hears.

"And then?" she asks cautiously. She wants more.

"Maybe a blindfold." A low chuckle escapes my chest. "If I take away another sense, your others may be heightened. Feel every breath, every touch."

"Mhmmm."

"And then," I continue, slow and deliberate, "I'd trail something cool against your skin. Maybe leather, maybe steel —you wouldn't know. That's the point."

Her lips part in a quiet exhale. "Daddy..."

"Already restless, baby? You haven't even felt anything yet."

Her back arches off the bed.

"Tell me," I coax gently, "would you trust me enough to let me choose what happens next?"

Aria remains quiet for a moment before whispering a breathy, "Yes."

"Go into the closet and grab a set of clamps and a vibrator." She does as she's told.

When she is back in the frame, I smile, seeing what she picked.

"Take off your clothes." Her eyes widen, but she continues to follow my instructions.

"Kneel."

She kneels in front of the camera, hands in her lap. She looks so perfect. My dick hardens seeing her like this, a perfect picture of submission.

"You're going to do as I say, and only as I say. Do you understand?"

She nods her head.

"Good girl. Turn the vibrator on." She hesitates, but does as she's told.

The buzzing is the only sound coming from her side of the phone.

"Use it, baby. Make yourself feel good."

I watch as she places it between her legs. Her body jolts as she finds her clit.

"You're doing so well, Aria." I unbuckle my belt as I watch her tilt her head back. My eyes trail down her neck to her chest, watching it rise and fall. Her breath hitches; she is getting close.

"Put it down." Her shoulders sink, but she does as she is told. "Take the clamps and put them on your nipples. She picked a pair that is connected by a chain. She places them gently, and the chain sways with her every movement. I reach into my pants and pull out my cock. It springs free of my waistband.

God, she is beautiful like this.

"How does that feel?"

"Good," she breathes out.

"Do you want to keep going?"

"Yes." Her voice is breathy.

My hand tightens around my cock as I begin to stroke up and down.

"Use your hands, baby. Show me how you make yourself cum." I swallow hard as I watch her slowly slide her hand between her legs. My dick twitches watching her fingers disappear inside of her, to reemerge, covered in her own mess. She slides her fingers around her clit and slowly begins to build up pressure.

"Such a good listener. Tell me something. What was something in the closet that sparked your interest?" I want to hear what she wants. Tell her how I can make those desires real. She begins to slow down her fingers as she is thinking of how to respond. "Don't stop, baby."

Her chest rises as she takes a deep breath, causing the chain to move.

"The cuffs and rope." I smile. She is testing the waters with something she already knows she enjoys.

"You like being bound to the bed?"

"Yes." Her cheeks redden when she answers.

"How about if your wrist were in cuffs, attached to the headboard, and I used a spreader on your legs?" I swallow as I grip my dick tighter at the thought of Aria exposed and vulnerable before me.

"Mhmm," she moans as she begins to move her hand faster.

"The way I can force you to orgasm, repeatedly, and you would be completely at my mercy."

I watch as she tries to hide the stutter in her breathing.

"What else, baby? What else did you see?" There are so many things in that closet, some of my favorites to bring out, others I've tried but don't revisit often. I want to see what she gravitated towards. I want to see what got her heart racing. What distracted her so much that she missed the check-in.

"You have plugs."

"I do."

"I've never..." she trails off, sliding her fingers further down her center before pressing them inside again.

"Never what?"

"I've never done anything like that."

"But you want to?" She takes a moment to answer before nodding her head.

"You're doing so well, Aria." I praise.

"Daddy," she breathes, reaching for the vibrator. "May I?"

"Yes, Baby." She grabs it and turns it back on, pressing it to her clit while she keeps her other fingers inside.

"We can start slow, introduce the plugs, have them in while we do some sensation play. Work up to wearing them during full scenes, or let you feel what it's like to be filled in all of your holes at the same time."

She bucks her hips at the idea, and I savor the way her body is reacting to the idea of us doing some of these things.

"Anything else you want to explore?" She remains quiet, riding the pleasure of the silicone vibrator between her thighs. "Did you see the paddles?"

She nods her head.

"And the canes?" She bites her lip. "The flogger?"

"Yes."

"The things that can cause pain." Her first question was

about pain, but none of the toys she brought up included pain. In the dressing room, her body reacted to being spanked. These must be the things that scare her, or the fact that she wants it scares her.

"Were those curiosity or fear?"

"Both."

"You're being so honest, Baby. Thank you for trusting me." I watch as her entire body relaxes. "Do you think you can trust me to introduce some of those toys? Help you experience the pleasure that can come from pain? To see my marks left on your body and feel the soreness days later?"

She bucks her hips against the vibrator. While she hasn't answered, her body is telling me what I need to know. We will need to have a more official negotiation conversation later, but she is interested.

I swallow a moan as precum coats my hand. I grip the head of my cock before pumping roughly several times. Tension coils in my abs.

"Eyes on me," I instruct, and she immediately brings her eyes back to the screen.

I place the phone on the top of the dresser. I want to show her exactly what she is doing to me.

"Baby, just the idea of you trusting me to explore these desires has me about to cum." My hand wraps tighter around my shaft. I continue to stroke myself, repeating how beautiful she is when she submits. Taking a staggered breath, I pump my wrist until the tension snaps, and I cum.

She watches, eyes wide, as I moan, "Aria," spilling myself down the front of my pant leg.

I step closer to the phone. "Do you want to cum, too, Aria?"

"Please, Daddy." She presses the vibrator harder against her clit.

"Then don't be late for proof of life." I smile. "Turn it off, baby." She does as she's told, but she isn't hiding any of her disappointment and anger.

"You have homework. I'm going to send you a worksheet. Fill it out before I get home." She huffs and rolls her eyes. I only smile in return.

Good. Be mad. Maybe next time you will follow the rules.

CHAPTER
Seven

ARIA

"Good afternoon, Ms. Mason. You look lovely today."

"Thank you, Enzo. I have an interview."

"I would say good luck, but you won't need it." He smiles at me. Over the last few days, I have really enjoyed getting to meet him. He has told me about his wife of forty-two years and their two grown children. He was so proud to tell me his youngest got into Pearson's School of Design. We laughed over coffee when my online order accidentally doubled.

Mia hasn't been back since our day of shopping, but she has made sure to text me every day. I'm starting to feel at home here. While on the outside that seems great, a fear is settling in my stomach that this all can be taken away in a minute. The fact that Theo isn't home yet doesn't make that fear any less. When he left, he said he would be gone for a night, two max. But now it seems like he will be gone for a week or more. Which is fine, work is work, and it's how he's able to afford the luxuries he is freely giving me, but not giving me any information about where he is or why his trip got extended is worrisome.

Is he with another woman? Is he extending his trip because he doesn't want to come home and kick me out? He would tell me if he didn't want me here, wouldn't he?

A black SUV pulls up, and the doorman opens the door for me. Between Theo and this level of service, I don't think I will ever touch another door handle. Sliding onto the seat, I ask the driver, who I learned is named Stan—unmarried, no kids, but does like walking through Central Park—to take me to the Castin Tower. They have their office located in one of the most well-known buildings they have built. It's very reminiscent of The Shard in London. I have always wondered if they intended to have it look like a particular superhero's tower, but either way, it is still a gorgeous piece of architecture.

As we pull up in front of the building, I note how the sun's light bounces off the glass and almost spotlights the buildings around it. Stan gets out and opens my door, assisting me onto the street.

"Thank you. I'll see you in a few." I smile as he tips his head.

"Just send me a message when you're ready to be picked up I'll be nearby." I smile before turning to enter the building. Another doorman is at the door, waiting for me, and ushers me inside.

"Ms. Mason, Mr. Castin has been expecting you. Please head up this elevator to the seventy-fifth floor." I look at my watch, a brand new Rolex I bought with Theo's money, to see if I am late. I arrived fifteen minutes early, like planned. I guess they really were expecting me. I head into the elevator as instructed and make my way to the correct floor.

The elevator beeps as it stops, the doors sliding open. I walk out into a beautifully decorated foyer. A petite woman behind the desk stands and smiles as I enter.

"Ms. Mason, it's nice to meet you." I smile, walking towards her to shake her hand. "I am Steph Davidson, Mr. Castin's assistant. He is finishing up with a call and will be out momentarily. Can I get you a bottle of water?" I gather that if I were to get hired, she would most likely be my boss, so I need to impress her just as much as I need to impress Mr. Castin.

"Sure, that would be great," I nervously respond. I have never received this type of treatment before a job interview. She walks back behind her desk and pulls a cold water bottle from underneath. Just as she hands me the bottle, a man walks around the corner of her desk.

"Aria Mason." He smiles like he is greeting a friend. "It's so great to meet you." He stretches out his hand, and I do the same for a handshake.

"It's such an honor to meet you. Your designs were consistently used in lectures at Acadia. You have designed some of the most beautiful buildings," I start to ramble before cutting myself off. He just smiles, as if this is a normal occurrence for him.

"Shall we?" he says, gesturing to the hall he came from.

"Yes, sir." I smile as he leads me toward a conference room.

He has me sit in a black leather office chair before he sits in a similar seat at the head of the table. He opens a black portfolio and pulls out a few pieces of paper.

"Mr. Reeves said you were new to the city?"

"Yes, I moved up here this weekend." I smile.

"What convinced you to do that?"

A man twice my age that fucks me better than anyone I've ever slept with before kind of kidnapped me with the promise of a better life.

"I was convinced to start over, get a fresh start, and make a name for myself outside of where I grew up." Not a lie, but I definitely can't give the actual answer.

"A great reason to move. Rough childhood?"

"Something like that, but it made me the hard worker I am today." He smiles.

"And why Castin? What makes you think we are the right place for you to make your name?"

"I recently graduated with my Bachelor's of Architecture, and believe this would be an amazing place to learn as I am working towards accreditation. Hopefully one day I can move up the ladder from receptionist to intern to designer."

"Bachelors?"

"From Acadia University, Suldatrian," I answer.

"We were not informed of that. Why did you not apply for our internship this year?"

"I had attempted to, but there were some...family issues." I try not to wince at the memory.

"If you're comfortable, can you elaborate?"

"One of your requirements is handwritten letters of recommendation. I had collected all of mine to mail in, but before I was able to put them in the mail, my mother accidentally shredded them with her sensitive documents." I try to keep my voice steady, but I'm not sure I'm succeeding. "And with the time it would take to reach back out to my advisors, I would not have made the deadline."

"I'm starting to understand the rough childhood."

"You don't even know half of it." I sigh, but then reach into my own portfolio and pull out some paperwork I printed off in Theo's office last night. "But I did bring my unofficial transcripts as well as photos of the letters of recommendation I received." He quickly takes them and looks them over.

"We have the handwritten requirement in there because we want to make sure the letters we are receiving are not a copy-paste version that a professor gives to every student. We also want to see if you left a big enough impression on these authority figures that they are willing to sit down and spend time writing out a letter for you by hand. From what I am seeing with these letters, not only were you an amazing student, but someone that these experts saw excelling in the field." He looks up from the paperwork. "And some of the names you've got to write these letters are some of the notoriously tough professors, ones who don't usually write recommendation letters for anyone."

"Acadia was where I got to thrive after years of being put in a box. I didn't want to waste that opportunity."

"I am glad you didn't." He taps the stack of papers back into a pile before handing them back to me. "I am surprised Theo didn't include this information."

"I don't think he knows. I mean, we haven't discussed much about my career."

"Don't underestimate him. He doesn't let many people into his inner circle. The fact that you are here means he trusts you; he probably did an extensive background check on you the night you met." Mr. Castin laughs knowingly. Everyone keeps saying Theo doesn't trust people, that he doesn't let anyone in, but he let me in, he practically pulled me in himself.

"I don't think the receptionist position is the right fit for you." My attention snaps back to the conversation at hand as my heart sinks to my stomach. "This year's internship program started two weeks ago. If you think you can catch up, we would like to add you to this year's roster. If your paperwork had been mailed in, you would have been offered the position."

I stare at him in shock for what feels like an eternity.

"Yes, absolutely. I can make up the two weeks quickly and can come in on weekends—" I stammer off until I'm interrupted.

"That won't be necessary." He laughs. "There is an intern proposal due next week; you will be expected to have it in with everyone else, even though they have had two weeks to complete it."

"Yes, sir. No problem, I would just need the client file, and I'll have it done ASAP." My smile reaches from ear to ear. I was ecstatic to be interviewing here for any job, but now I'm leaving with an internship at one of the most prestigious firms in the city. I did this. Theo may have gotten me an interview, but I earned this spot with my hard work. I am so glad I thought to take pictures of my recommendation letters as I received them. Those recommendations got me this job. I should send all my professors fruit baskets.

"We can get that to you today, but let's get you to HR first and get your paperwork all set up. You can start tomorrow at eight a.m."

"I'll be here." We walk out of his office and into the elevator. We exit on the seventy-third floor.

He knocks on a glass door, and a young man stands up from behind his desk.

"Malcom, this is Aria Mason. She will be joining us in the internship program this year." He looks at Mr. Castin with confusion. "Since she is starting later than the rest, we really need her paperwork completed today so she can start tomorrow." His attention shifts to me. "Malcolm Williams is the head of HR here at Castin Construction and will get you taken care of. Once you are done here, he will shoot me a message and I will show you to your desk and have you meet the other interns." I nod as Malcom offers me a chair.

"I take it the interview went well." He laughs.

"You could say that." The smile still hasn't left my face.

"Please give me just a moment. I was preparing to hire a receptionist, not an intern, so I need to adjust a few things." He starts typing as his phone dings. He looks at the message before returning his attention to the computer screen. "I think well is an understatement."

"What do you mean?" I ask. Now I want to know what message he received.

"Kai, I mean Mr. Castin, has sent over the offer letter, and is offering you a salary reserved for a select few interns."

"Oh, really? Can I see?" I completely forgot I was going to get paid for this job. I was willing to accept any salary, but being told I am getting a really good offer is exciting.

"Absolutely. Let me get it printed off. If you accept these terms, I will need you to sign the letter, and we can get your contract drawn up."

He spins his chair around and grabs a paper off the printer behind him.

He slides it over to me, and as I look down, something finally takes the smile off my face.

My jaw has hit the floor looking over the salary.

"Are you sure this is correct?" I look up to Malcom.

"Triple checked." He smiles.

"Do you have a p—" He has a pen held out for me before I can finish asking the question. Of course he did—who in their right mind would turn down a 100k a year entry-level salary? I have heard rumors that Castin Construction pays well and takes care of its people. But this is 25k better than other junior architect jobs, and I'm only an intern. I can only go up from here. I really need to send my professors a gift basket, especially now that I can afford it. Well, I'll still use Theo's card, but that's not the point.

I sign all the necessary paperwork, and Mr. Castin does as he said he would and meets me at the elevator to take me to my desk.

"Here is the intern's section of the office. We have you all together so you can collaborate. Here is where you will be. Jonathan is to your right, and Abigail is in front of you. They should be able to get you up to speed. The client folder is on your desk for the proposal due next Friday. The interns should be getting out of a meeting in a few minutes, and there is only about an hour left in the work day, so if you would like to stay and meet the team, you are more than welcome. Or you can head home, and we will see you tomorrow."

Mr. Castin leans on my desk with his hands in his pockets. I can't help but notice how attractive he is. His tousled, brown hair, the perfect amount of scruff, the way when he looks at me, his eyes look almost black. Definitely my type, but even though he is objectively hot, he's not stirring any feelings. I think Theo has ruined me. I mean I am sitting next to an extremely attractive man, and all I want is to call Theo and tell him about my day.

I'm totally fucked.

I mean we aren't even really officially anything other than kinky fuck buddies. I am going to be devastated when he ends things.

"I'd like to stay and meet the team." I smile, crossing my

arms and looking around the office. It's huge. I guess if you're designing a building you know you're going to be in, you're going to make it perfect.

"Sounds good." He looks toward what I am assuming is a conference room where a door just opened. "Perfect timing. They are all headed this way."

Several people quickly find their desks and sit down to take notes. A curly-headed blonde woman sits at the desk in front of me, I am going to assume that she is the Abigail I was told about.

"Hey, Mr. Castin, to what do we owe the pleasure?" A dirty blond haired man walks over to the desk next to me. This must be Johnathon. For some reason, I immediately want to keep my distance. I get a very my *dad's a lawyer* vibes from him.

All the interns' attention shoots up in our direction.

"Everyone, I would like to introduce you to Aria Mason. She is the final intern joining this year's roster. There was an incident with her paperwork which kept her from joining us, but now that we have it squared away, she is going to play a little catch up and be a great addition to the team. Please make her feel welcome." Some of the eyes staring at me are welcoming and approachable, others are very upset that I am here. Abigail seems happy to see me, while the only other female intern is shooting daggers at me. The guys are either smiling or indifferent. Then there is Jonathan. He is already walking towards me to introduce himself. Confidence does not seem to be something he lacks. I put my focus on Abigail and introduce myself, she seems nice. A little quiet, but nice. I can work with nice.

Jonathan interrupts and immediately starts offering to help me catch up. I cannot help but roll my eyes.

"I appreciate the offer, but I think your attention is going to be better suited if focused on your own proposal." I turn back to my desk and open my client file. I can hear Mr. Castin laugh as he turns away. "Mr. Castin?"

"Yes?"

"Thank you for introducing me to the team. If it is ok with you, I would like to take this file home and get started on it."

"Absolutely, we will see you tomorrow at eight." He smiles.

"Absolutely. I am excited to be a part of this team. If I have any questions or concerns about this proposal, who would you like me to direct my questions to?"

"Just shoot me an email. I would be happy to help you get up to speed."

I thank him and he walks out with me.

"Thank you so much for today, I am very excited to be on your team."

"We are excited to have you. Give Theo hell for me, he definitely buried the lead with you."

I smile as he holds the elevator door open for me. "I will."

As I walk into the lobby, I pull out my phone to call Stan, but I hear my name being shouted. I look up and see Mia near the doors with a huge smile on her face.

"Congratulations, girl! Let's go celebrate!" She wraps her arms around me, giving me the biggest hug.

CHAPTER
Eight

ARIA

Ms. Davidson had texted Mia when Mr. Castin escorted me to HR, so Mia immediately made reservations for us to celebrate. Of course, dinner was phenomenal. It was really nice to have someone to celebrate with. I wish Theo were home to celebrate with, but Mia was a great stand-in.

I look at the time, 8:45 p.m.

"Thank you so much for dinner. I need to head upstairs, but we need to do this again soon." I hug her before she leaves.

I head upstairs and sit in the living room, knowing any minute now I'll be getting a call or text from Theo.

Like clockwork, the clock strikes nine, and my phone rings.

"Hey, Daddy."

"How did it go today?" he asks immediately. I would have thought he would already know. He's close friends with the CEO who interviewed me today, and apparently, everyone's assistants know each other and gossip.

"I didn't get the receptionist job," I say, trying to hide the excitement in my voice.

"No?" he asks, somehow knowing.

"No, but I did get an internship position." The excitement is barely contained.

"Congratulations, baby girl, I knew you could do it."

"So you knew I graduated with honors and had my degree?"

"Salutatorian. You graduated salutatorian, don't downplay that."

"You did your homework on me!" *What else does this man know?*

"Yes, I did, the night we met," he says so matter-of-factly.

"Why?" What about me made him run home and background check on me?

"It started as curiosity, you were Alana's daughter, and I wanted to know more about the girl with the most vibrant green eyes, who let me watch the mascara run from her eyes while she was on her knees for me."

"So you wanted to look into your ex and know who you fucked." Not really the response I wanted.

"I also wanted to know more about the girl I couldn't get out of my mind. I thought you were off limits. I thought once you found out who I was, you would want nothing to do with me."

"But you still came to the bar that night."

"I did. There is just something about you, something I don't want to lose."

"So when I told you about Dodd, did you already know?"

"No, I only did a criminal background check and had your social media looked over."

"My social media? I don't post much."

"You don't, but you did post your graduation, holding your diploma." I did. That must be how he found out about my degree and my class rank.

"And a background check and look at my pictures was enough for you to feel like you could trust me?" If he really is as protective and secretive as everyone has told me he is, why did he trust me?

"That and the fact that when I asked you questions, you told me the truth. You didn't hide things or brush things off. You trusted me, too."

I did, and I still do. He has been in my life for days, and I already trust him more than the woman who raised me.

"So if you knew about my degree, why didn't you tell Mr. Castin?"

"If I had set up an interview for the internship position and you had gotten it, would you believe you deserved it?" I sit quietly for a minute before answering. I want to say yes, I would have, but is that true? I knew I was getting an interview as a favor to Theo; if I was told I was getting an interview for the internship as a favor to Theo, I would have thought that the job was also a favor.

"No," I finally respond.

"I gave you the opportunity to bring it up and brag about yourself. You earned that position, and that's why you have it. Not because of my friendship with Kai."

"But doesn't that look weird that you didn't tell your friend relevant information about your girlfriend?" The word slips out before I can stop it.

"Girlfriend? Is that what you said you were to me?" he taunts.

"No. I just—I just assumed that is how it looks. Is that ok? I mean, I can make it known that I'm not." Fuck. Theo doesn't let people in easily, and now I'm making assumptions and portraying us as something we are not. Theo's laugh pulls me back to the conversation.

"Baby, I didn't give him details about who you are to me. Honestly, it's none of his business. As you've figured out, I don't share much about myself with anybody."

"What about Eddie?" He is always receiving messages from him. Either they work really closely together, or they are friends.

"Unfortunately, yes. I do share things with Eddie, but he weaseled his way into my life. I'm choosing you, and choosing to share things with you." I let out a small sigh. Hearing his reassurance of wanting me here with him brings a sense of calm over my body. "Even though I am fairly private, I won't stop you from telling people about it and what we are. Whatever you're comfortable telling people."

"What are we?" I mean, I know we have entered a dynamic, but going around saying he's my dom is kind of weird. And just because we're fucking doesn't mean we're dating, but I do live with him.

"I am not sure. I haven't really done the relationship thing in a while. I don't want to rush anything, but also know we're more than friends."

"Roommates?"

"Baby, we're more than just roommates." We both laugh. I love how we're in a kind of important conversation, but still are comfortable enough to mess around a little bit.

"I mean, roommates are good."

"I don't have phone sex with my roommates."

"I mean, if I don't cum, is it still considered sex?" I tease. I still can't believe that's how he chose to punish me for missing proof of life, even though it was super hot.

"Aria." His voice is stern.

"Daddy." I mimic.

"You're asking for trouble."

"I don't think I'm asking." I laugh. This is one of my favorite parts of this dynamic. He acts like he doesn't like it, but he really does.

"You're going to regret this attitude when I come home."

"If you come home." At this point, I don't think he will be home anytime soon.

"When. *When* I come home. I have someone very special waiting for me."

"Eddie?"

"Definitely, not Eddie." He laughs. "Have you decided what we are yet?"

"Wait, it's my decision? I thought you were in control."

"This is one thing we decide together. Especially since I am not the one who will be having to tell people what we are to each other. "

"I guess we're dating, but I'm not going to broadcast that. I mean, you're absolutely right, it's no one's business but ours."

"Sounds good. I am very excited to come home to my girlfriend soon." The way he says it sends lightning to my core. He has almost exclusively called my baby or baby girl, but hearing him lay claim to me has me wishing he were here, or at least there wasn't a no orgasm rule.

"When will you be coming home?"

"Soon, we're about to handle a large part of the project. So I do have to go."

"Ok." My voice deflates. I miss him. I want him here. At minimum, I want to know why he is away for so long, but he only gives vague details. I can't even tell what his job is. Maybe I can get some information from Mr. Castin at work.

"Good night, baby. I'll talk to you tomorrow." The sound of a car door and shouting drowns out my response before the call ends.

I don't know what he's doing, but it did sound like a lot of secrets. Maybe I should figure out where I could go if this ends badly. He may have ruined other men for me, but that doesn't mean I will stay somewhere where I am consistently lied to, even if it is just lies of omission.

I open up my laptop, but instead of jumping into my client folder, I start searching for apartments near work that I qualify for with my new salary.

CHAPTER
Nine

ARIA

Using Theo's money to DoorDash breakfast has to be the best perk of using his money. You mean I can order breakfast while doing my makeup, and it will be downstairs waiting for me when I get into the car, a car I don't even have to drive? When this ends, I think this is what I'm going to miss most.

Like clockwork, Angie shows up with my coffee and bagel, just as Stan pulls the SUV in front of my building.

"Good Morning, Ms. Mason."

"Good Morning, Stan. Is Enzo not here today?" I didn't see him at his desk this morning. I have gotten used to him greeting me every morning.

"I will find out, but for now, let's get you to work. Don't want to be late on your first day." He opens the door and helps me in before closing the door and walking around the front of the vehicle.

The drive is uneventful, and before I have a chance to finish my coffee, we pull up to Castin Tower. Once out of the car, I walk into the foyer and run into Abigail.

"Do you always have a driver?" she asks, looking past me at Stan.

"Kind of, my boyfriend is extremely protective," I respond, realizing *boyfriend* came out so easily. I guess I am telling people.

"Oh." She pauses, making me think I said something wrong or that she is judging me for having access to money. "That's cool. Hey, did you get a chance to look over the client folder?"

"Yeah, I did." I relax as we chat about our proposals while getting into the elevator. By the time we get to our floor, most of the interns are already at their desks. I set my things down and continue my conversation with Abigail. Jonathan stands up and walks between our desks.

"Ladies, ladies, it is too early to be discussing such complicated topics. At least let me treat us to some coffee first."

"No thanks. I already had mine, since I came to work, to —what is it?" I look at Abigail, feigning to remember a word. "Right, work." I turn back to my new friend, who is clearly holding back a laugh. We continue our conversation, ignoring the fact that Johnathon is standing directly next to us. We head to the conference room for the morning meeting. As I sit down with Abigail and one of the guys, Tucker, I am asked where I went to school.

"I graduated from Acadia University as salutatorian." Tucker's eyes widen at the last word.

"Well, that explains it," a snarky voice from behind me speaks. We all turn to look at Elle.

"Explains what?" I ask. I can already tell Elle is going to be a problem.

"Why you were given an exemption."

"What exemption? What are you even talking about?"

"You were allowed to be an intern even though your paperwork wasn't in on time. They don't do that for everybody." I knew that, I assumed it was because of my qualifications and a little help from Theo. What does my alma mater have to do with it?

"Half the execs of Castin Construction went to Acadia. If you had graduated anywhere else, you wouldn't be here." She seems so proud of herself for figuring it out.

"Well, all that matters is I'm here now and did what took you three weeks in one night." I pull out my proposal and place it in front of me. I didn't technically do three weeks of work in one night, but this particular client had remarkable similarities to a project I completed in one of my courses. I was easily able to make a few simple adjustments and have a completed proposal. Mr. Castin walks in at that exact moment.

"Did I just hear you say your proposal is complete?" he asks as he stops behind me.

"Yes, I finished it last night. So, unless there is a part that was not given to me, it has been completed."

"Mind if I take a look?"

"Not at all." I hand him my portfolio. He flips through several pages.

"If any of you were wondering why she was allowed to start late, here is your answer. Being a graduate of Acadia may have gotten our attention, but this right here is why she has the job. This looks great, Aria. Later today, I'd like to set up a meeting to go over it and see where we can improve." Again, Mr. Castin has me smiling from ear to ear. His eyes look down at me, and all I can see is a gold shimmer I didn't see before.

He then walks to the head of the table and starts the meeting. A large group of men in suits, I believe to be the board of executives, walks past the conference room window. I look at all their faces, looking to see if I remember any of them. Did they come speak in any of my lectures? Did I see them at any alumni events? Did I speak with any at a networking event?

Once the meeting is over, we are excused back to our desks to work on our proposals. As I sit down to review it and take notes on things to improve for my meeting later, Elle walks up to my desk.

"I don't care that you're good at the job. You still shouldn't be here."

"It's a good thing your opinion doesn't matter then, does it? If you'll excuse me, I have work to do."

"It's not fair, we all started weeks ago after a grueling interview process. Do you understand that hundreds, if not thousands, of graduates apply, and they only take ten?"

"Eleven," I correct.

"No, ten."

I look around and count, "One, two, three, four, five, six, seven, eight, nine, ten," and point my finger at my chest, "eleven."

"They have never taken eleven before. So, I don't understand why they made an exception for *you*." Her emphasis was definitely supposed to be a jab.

"You don't need to understand; that is not your job. Your job is to finish that proposal. Maybe if you spent less time worrying about why I am here and used this time to do your actual job, you could be done and have a meeting with Mr. Castin today. But instead of doing the job you are paid to do, you are at my desk keeping me from doing mine." The crowd of interns is silent as they wait for Elle's response. She finally groans and walks away. Everyone goes back to their business except Abigail and Johnathon.

"She is just worried you threaten her spot," Abigail suggests.

"They added me, not replaced someone with me," I counter.

"I think she means for the full-time position." I look at Jonathan for more information. I know that a few interns are hired on after the year, but I don't understand how my being here changes anything.

"Yeah, they only hire three of us. And so it went from 3/10 to 3/11. And they have already shown that they favor you, giving you the exception to start late. So I think she is seeing it now as a twenty percent chance of getting hired at the end. Since you are probably guaranteed one."

"I'm not guaranteed anything," I argue.

"True, but you're kicking ass on day one, it's going to have to take a major fuck up for you to not be at the top of the intern ranking."

"Still plausible," I retort.

"Unlikely." Johnathon smiles.

"Improbable," Abigail retorts.

"Well, that's not my fault. If she works hard, I am sure she will be fine. Even if she doesn't get hired, she will have her pick of other companies that would literally be begging to hire her. This internship is a golden ticket."

"She doesn't want to work anywhere else." She pauses, looking at me like I just said she could work on Mars. "Her dad is on the board."

"Wait, what?" That is a plot twist.

"Her dad helped start the company. Going anywhere else would be considered a failure."

"Oh shit. But shouldn't she be the favorite for one of the spots then?"

"She was until you showed up," she explains.

"Oh, I get why she hates me now."

"Yeah," they both say in unison.

"It will be fine, she has a year to figure it out," Jonathan interjects, oblivious to the emotional roller coaster I am on. "But hey, a bunch of us interns are going to dinner tonight. Want to come?"

"Will Elle be there?" I really don't want to have to deal with snide comments all evening.

"Probably not if you come." I drop my face into my hands.

"Sure, I will come."

"Ms. Mason, can I speak with you?" Ms. Davidson interrupts.

"Absolutely," I answer before walking to her desk.

CHAPTER
Ten

THEO

"If they can't handle it, we will have to assign someone to it. This shouldn't be out of their scope of skills." This trip was longer than expected, and there were still some issues to figure out, but I needed to come home. "Is there anyone we can move and not cause issues elsewhere?" Eddie is concerned we left too soon. I told him he could stay behind and run things, but I was leaving.

"I have full confidence in the Raiden boys. I don't think we will have to move anybody, plus they have the support of Acadia being nearby. This shouldn't be an issue."

"Sir, we are two blocks away," William interrupts.

"Eddie, I have to go. We can finish this discussion later."

"Ok, Daddy. I'll set up a meeting." My jaw tightens as he talks.

"How long are you going to keep this up?" I asked, gritted through my teeth.

"Until it doesn't annoy you anymore." He laughs. "Is it just the age gap thing? Because we're what, ten years apart?

That's still an age gap, so it makes sense I get to call you Daddy, too."

"No, it's not—never mind." I cut myself off before I give him anything else to use against me.

"Oh, so it is a sex thing!" *And...I was too late.*

"Eddie, I'm hanging up now."

"Ok. Bye, Daddy." His laugh gets cut off when I hang up.

We pull up in front of Castin Tower. The moment the car stops, I am out the door. The doorman barely has time to react before I am barreling through the glass doors.

"Mr. Reeves, how may I assist you today?"

"Let Mr. Castin know I am on my way up." I continue walking to the elevator I know takes me directly to the CEO's office.

I hear a "Yes, sir," and the scrambling of a phone behind the counter as I enter the elevator. For seventy-five floors, the ride is quick. I enter the office just as Kai puts the phone down. He leans back in his chair, watching me.

"Always did have a flair for the dramatic." He laughs.

"What's the point of having a reputation like mine if I don't get to wield it?" I laugh, pulling my jacket off. I have known Kai for just over twenty years. He was who introduced me to The Society, and is a huge reason I am the person I am today. He stands to shake my hand before offering me a seat.

"Can I offer you a drink?" He pulls scotch off one of the shelves behind him.

"Sure." Taking the glass, I sit back in the seat. "How is she doing?" Kai has a knowing smile as he relaxes back into his seat.

"She's doing great. You didn't tell us she graduated second in her class with a Bachelor's of Architecture."

"I did not." I smile into my glass as I raise it to my lips, knowing where this is going.

"And why is that? You must have background checked her if she has gotten this close to you. You would have known she had her degree from Acadia, of all places. It seems like pertinent information when asking us to do you a favor."

"I only asked you to interview her; you chose to hire her on your own."

"True, and we probably would have given her a low-stakes job just to keep you happy."

"But you decided to bend rules for her." I smile, knowing that they see the strong, capable, and smart woman I do.

"Did you see who recommended her?"

"I did not." If he is impressed, it has to be someone influential.

"Sebastian Thorne. Have anything to do with that?"

"Nope, didn't even know she was in his class. We didn't meet until after she graduated." His eyes widen. We went to school with Sebastian; he was the first of us to find out about The Court. He has done well for himself, with the help of the Knights.

"So you have only known each other for a few months?" He smiles, feeling like he has uncovered some huge secret. Just because I don't tell everyone everything doesn't mean I'm hiding things. I mean, I do hide things, but Aria will never be one of them. "She had said she moved here this weekend. Have anything to do with that?"

"Obviously. I couldn't leave her again."

"But you left this weekend to go back to Acadia?"

"That's different."

"So did you date before and then rekindle? Wait, that wouldn't make sense if you met her after she graduated." He takes a sip of his scotch before trying to piece the puzzle back together.

"How long are you planning on interrogating me about my relationship?"

"Until it makes sense. I do appreciate you admitting it's a relationship, though."

"Would I ask for a favor for just anyone?"

"You never ask for favors."

"Exactly."

A knock on the office door pulls our attention. Ms. Davidson pokes her head in.

"Good to see you, Mr. Reeves. Mr. Castin, the interns will be leaving their end-of-day meeting soon. If you needed to tell them anything before they leave for the evening, now would be the time."

"Thank you, Steph. We will head over there momentarily."

I finish off the last of the scotch in my glass before placing it down on his desk. He continues to watch me as we head to the interns' desks, practically taking notes to see if any changes in my body language will crack the code.

The desks are all full, except one. It seems the guy who sits next to Aria feels the need to lean all over her desk. Heat rises into my chest. *Who the fuck is this guy, and why is he that close to my girl?*

"Jealousy. This is serious." Kai laughs.

"She won't be in tomorrow."

"She has things to do, tasks to complete."

"She can do them from home," I growl before pushing past him to Aria's desk. As I get closer, I can start to hear the conversation between Aria and the guy, who, if he doesn't back off, will be found in a ditch.

"Still good for dinner and drinks tonight?" he asks.

She is going on a date? Didn't she just push for a title? She can't be serious.

"Ye—" She starts to respond, but I cut her off.

"She has plans." Her head whips around in surprise. Not a surprise of getting caught, but one of excitement. She is smiling ear to ear. In a blink, she is up out of her chair and in my arms. I pull her in close, and when she lifts her face to mine, I cannot help but pull her lips against mine. She lowers herself off her tiptoes, smiling up at me.

She looks over her shoulder at *whatever his name is,* who is just staring at us. "Yes, I will still be at dinner."

"No, you won't," I growl.

"You weren't home and couldn't tell me when you would be, so I made plans."

"With another man? If I didn't make it clear, baby, I don't share."

"It is most of the interns celebrating my joining the team. It won't be too long, promise," she explains, and I do feel slightly better knowing she won't be alone with this fraternity reject.

I lean down, placing my lips against her ear.

"If you want to go to dinner with your friends, that's fine, but know I haven't stopped thinking of each and every way I am going to make you cum using the things you found in my closet. I want to play, and I don't like being kept waiting." I can hear her breath catch as she listens to my soft words. "The longer I am left to wait, the harder it is going to be to earn my forgiveness."

She lets out the softest moan. I pull away from her, smiling, knowing my words are affecting her body. She may be masking it well while we're in public, but I can see it. We may have to do this again sometime. I like watching her fight to hide what is happening.

"I will see you later. Enjoy your dinner." I kiss the top of her head before walking away. Kai is still watching us from the hallway.

"Interesting," is all he says as he leads me out of the building.

CHAPTER
Eleven

ARIA

 Luckily, the place we all decided on for dinner is just up the street. I stay back while Abigail packs up the last of her things. Everyone left a few minutes ago to head to dinner, and as predicted, when Elle found out I was invited, she huffed and walked away. The office is almost empty, so I'm a little surprised when Mr. Castin walks over.

 "Ms. Mason, I'm glad I was able to catch you. Can you please make sure to take home anything necessary for you to work from home tomorrow?"

 "Work from home?" I ask, genuinely confused.

 "Yes. There was a request put in, and it was approved since you have caught up and surpassed some of your colleagues. We don't see a reason not to allow it. "

 "I didn't put in any request." I don't even know how to request time off, let alone remote work.

 "Well, it has already been approved. So we aren't expecting you tomorrow. You may as well take the day." His smile hides something. He walked out with Theo earlier. Did he have something to do with this? Is he really expecting me to not come to work tomorrow?

My mind immediately wanders to what he said to me before he left.

I am going to make you cum using the things you found in my closet. I want to play, and I don't like being kept waiting. The longer I am left to wait, the harder it is going to be to earn my forgiveness.

Heat pools in my stomach thinking about what he has planned, and how he has planned ahead for me to not have to come to work tomorrow. He is expecting this to take a long time, and I am going to need time to recover. This is just another way he is trying to take care of me.

"Ok, I guess I'll pack up a few files, and I will get them done at home tomorrow." I look at Abigail, who seems to be just as confused as I am. I am taking it that this is not something done often with interns.

"Perfect. Ms. Tagle, I would also like to extend the offer to you. Would you like to work remotely tomorrow?" Abigail's eyes widen.

"Are you sure?"

"Absolutely. I looked over your proposal and am very impressed with the concepts you decided to pitch. I'll be setting up a meeting on Friday to discuss the reasoning behind your choices." Abigail takes the praise and just nods her head.

"Thank you, that would be amazing."

"Perfect, I will have Ms. Davidson note it in our systems. You both will still be responsible for tomorrow's work, but enjoy doing it from home."

"Thank you," we both say in unison before letting out a soft laugh. Mr. Castin leaves before Abigail turns to me.

"He has never let interns work from home. Did you really put in a request?"

"I didn't, but I think I may know what happened." I laugh and try to brush it off, hoping she won't ask many more questions. "Do you need me to make a copy of the Branson file?"

"No, I already have a copy. Jonathan asked for it, but never came to get it. I guess this is my copy now." We both laugh.

After packing our things, we make it downstairs where Johnathon is waiting outside.

"Took you ladies long enough." He sighs.

"We didn't ask you to wait. Mr. Castin stopped by the desks before we left."

"Really? What did he need?"

"He told us we were allowed to work from home tomorrow, and made sure we were able to pack up everything we would need." Abigail smiles. I just nod along, appreciative that she didn't make it seem like I was singled out again.

"Fuck, next time I am waiting for you guys upstairs. I would kill to be able to work from my bed." He grumbles a little but doesn't ask any more questions about it.

We all walk together to the restaurant a block down, and Abigail heads up the stairs to the bar as Johnathon pulls me to the side. "Hey, want to share a cigarette before we head up?"

"I don't smoke," I reply. Abigail already halfway up the stairs. Jonathan watches as she turns the corner.

"I know." He looks down at his shoes and takes a breath before looking at me. I just stand there, confused as to why he would ask to smoke if he knew I didn't. "I just wanted to ask you something alone."

Is he really going to ask me out even after seeing I'm with someone else?

"The guy from earlier, your boyfriend?"

"Yeah..." I answer tentatively.

"You're not going to get in trouble when you go home tonight, right?" His voice is full of concern.

I just stare at him for a second, unsure of how to answer or why he would even ask.

"He just seemed a little..." he pauses.

"Older?" I offer.

"Yes, but no. He seemed a little controlling? Maybe even a little aggressive. I just want to make sure that he's not going to hurt you when you go home."

Hurt me? Yes, please. Knowing Theo, if he is planning on delivering pain, it will be coupled with equal amounts of pleasure. He gets off on others trusting him to provide those unconventional desires. While it may hurt, and I hope it does, it is only fun if we both enjoy it.

"No, he won't, I won't," I stammer unconvincingly. I take a breath. "Thank you for your concern, but I can promise I am safe." I reach out and touch his arm. He may be a stereo-typical frat boy, but seeing him actually be concerned for my safety is sweet. I would still never touch him with a ten-foot pole on a regular occasion, but this side of him is nice.

He shakes his head and nods before leading us toward the stairs.

"Aren't you going to smoke?"

"Nope, I don't smoke either." I nod, realizing he just needed to find an excuse to hold us back a second. Maybe he isn't such a bad guy. Annoying, sure, but he seems to have a good heart. I hope it stays that way.

We make it up to the table, and everyone is ordering their

drinks. By the time the waiter gets to us, I have figured out my order.

"And for you?"

"French 76, please."

"Do you mean French 75?"

"No, I want vodka instead of gin. Is that possible?"

"Absolutely." He nods, then looks to Jonathan, who just orders a rum and Coke.

Abigail saved us seats at the end of the table next to Tucker and Peter.

"Did Castin really say you could work from home tomorrow, or is Abigail pulling one over on us?" Peter leans over the table so I can hear him.

"No, apparently a request got put in and he approved it. Then extended the offer to Abigail when I told him I didn't make a request." The boys looked shocked. "And we decided not to look a gift horse in the mouth and accepted, packed up our stuff, and left."

"He said it was because he was impressed with my proposal, and we all know he loved Aria's. Has anyone else finished theirs and turned it in for review?" The boys look around the table before looking back at us and shaking their heads.

"No one else?"

"We have until Friday. Why would we turn it in early?"

"To impress the guy we want to hire us at the end of the year?" Abigail sasses back. She is definitely more open outside of work. I can admire that skill. Women already have to work harder than men in almost any career; why give them anything else to critique or use against her? At work, it's all business, but at the bar with us, she's definitely letting those curls down.

The bar is filled with conversations and laughter. The table is full of friendly debates and rivalry. I sit back and watch as a group of people, all competing for the same job, put that aside and still have a good time together. Maybe it's because they are men that they don't have the same rivalry, but this thing with Elle—I don't see how it can have a happy ending. Even if we both get hired on together, there will always be a rivalry and jealousy. It is not going to end well.

I take a sip from my glass as my phone vibrates. I look down to see a message from Theo.

I am still waiting.

The message is simple, but has huge implications. I smile down at it, picturing Theo in the guest room pulling out his toys and deciding what he is going to use on me tonight. A moment later, my phone buzzes again.

Did you want to add anything to your homework?

Homework? What homework?

?

Your hard limits. That worksheet you filled out.

No.

You can change your mind.

I know, I don't want to. I don't know what is going to be too much. I want to find those limits with you.

Come home.

I will.

Now.

When I'm done.

Should I be pushing buttons when I am already pushing a boundary, making him wait? Probably not, but I really want to know what he has planned for me tonight.

Abigail asks for my opinion to settle a debate, and I am pulled into the wild conversation at the table.

Even while watching Peter and Tucker have a heated debate about which design came first, Stark Tower or Castin Tower, there is a little voice in the back of my head saying *Go home to Theo.*

I swallow the last of my drink and take out my phone.

Can you send a car, please?

Stan has been outside since you got off work.

You made him sit out there this entire time?

It's his job.

I'll be home soon.

I'll be waiting.

Closing the phone, I flag down the waiter.

"I am going to be heading home. I will see you all on Thursday." The boys give me a hard time about working from home tomorrow, but Johnathon just watches without comment. When we make eye contact, I mouth the words *I am safe, promise.* He just nods before downing the rest of his drink.

I grab my bag and head downstairs, and like Theo had said, Stan is standing out front holding my door open.

"Sorry for making you wait."

"It's quite all right, Ms. Mason."

He closes the door, and for a brief moment, the air around me is still and silent. I take a deep breath, finally admitting to myself what I may have caused myself to walk into at home. Well, at Theo's home.

When he FaceTimed me that first night, he said so many things. He told me all about how he would use certain toys, how he wanted to leave marks across my body. The conversation was so hot. But a lot of things can be hot when it's just words. He is about to actually do those things to me. A knot forms in my stomach and battles the heat rising from my core as I start to remember all the things he had said he wanted to do.

The logical part of my brain keeps telling me it's dangerous, that I should be scared. But on the other hand, it's telling me that I want it. All of it. That the fear is fun, like a haunted house. We pay to go be scared. We pay to have our nervous system attacked and us put into fight or flight.

Theo would never intentionally hurt me—I don't think. At least he wouldn't hurt me if I didn't want it. He has been very intentional about making sure I understand this is an agreement between both of us. That there are hard limits, and even when we were together before, if he introduced anything that could make me uncomfortable, he made sure I knew I could say no and how to say no.

I trace my fingers over the spot on my wrist where Theo had bound me to the bed.

My attention is pulled back to reality when Stan opens the door. I hadn't even realized we had started the drive home. *It's now or never.* I step out of the car. Stan tries to hand me my bag.

"Can you leave that with Enzo? Have him send it up in the morning?"

"Yes, ma'am."

I take the elevator up and enter the foyer to the penthouse. Once inside the door, all the lights are off. Except one in Theo's room.

I slowly make my way to the open door, counting my steps. My heart pounds in my ears as my core tightens. The mix of want and fear battles as I inch closer step by step. Once in the doorway, I can see Theo sitting on the couch at the foot of his bed.

"Daddy?" I ask softly.

"Explain the stop lights."

"Red means stop, Yellow means approaching red, check in, or slow down. Green means good to go."

"And you will use them."

"If I need to." I smile as I see his hand flex over his knee.

He looks at me, his eyes dark. He has been waiting all night for this, for me.

"Come here."

"Yes, Daddy." I slowly walk to him, taking in every moment his eyes shift over my body.

I stand in front of him. He places his hands on my hips before standing, towering over me.

"Strip."

CHAPTER
Twelve

ARIA

"Strip."

My core tightens at his command. I slide my feet out of my heels and kick them off to the side. I maintain eye contact the entire time I am unbuckling my belt and sliding my pants down my legs.

Theo's expression doesn't change, his eyes don't wander. His gaze remains fixed on mine.

I pull my shirt over my head, leaving me in just the black lace bra he purchased for me the night before he left.

Slowly unhooking it, it slides down my arms to the floor.

"Give me your wrists." I bring them in front of my body and offer them to Theo. This is becoming almost a ritual. Not that I am complaining, but it's become a familiar routine. He removes my watch before securing my wrists in the cuffs.

I expect him to carry me to the bed, but he doesn't. He turns me around and bends me over the side of the bed. He attaches the cuffs to a leash attached to the headboard. He pushes my legs apart and puts cuffs on them as well. I stand on my tippy toes, and I am unable to close my legs. He steps back and watches as I adjust to this new position. Even though I have been bound and naked with Theo before, this somehow feels different, more vulnerable. There is nowhere to hide. No way to pull away. I am truly at his mercy.

He seems to enjoy this very fact. I try to look over my shoulder and watch him as he sits back on the couch, arms resting on the top of the couch, in his lap is a long, thin, black stick with a leather flap on the end. It was hanging next to the flogger and paddle, so I can only assume it serves the same purpose.

My heart begins to quicken in anticipation. I stare at the whip in his lap. My chest tightens, but so does my core.

"Aria." Theo pulls my attention to him. "Do you know how long you made me wait?"

"No." I could guess, but I am not sure. I drop my head into the sheets, knowing if I fight to keep my head up, my neck is going to be extremely sore.

"Nearly three hours." That can't be right. I tried to remember what the time I saw on my watch or clock was, but couldn't. "So now it's your turn to try and earn forgiveness."

I hear Theo stand off the couch. He walks around, admiring me. He stops behind me and places the end of the whip on the back of my neck. He slowly drags it down my spine. My breath hitches. My core tightens as he keeps lowering it down my back and stops with it gently placed along my ass crack.

While my brain is telling me I am in danger and to be scared, trying to trigger my fight or flight, my pussy is drenched.

Theo lifts the leather off my body then snaps it. I let out a surprised yelp as my body jumps at the sound of it making contact. For a brief minute, I couldn't tell if he made contact with me or the bed.

I look to the side of me to see the whip still sitting where Theo had snapped it, against the bed.

I take a deep breath, contemplating the mixture of relief and disappointment swirling in my chest.

"Don't worry, baby. Your turn will come. Just not yet." Theo smiles as he puts the whip back on the couch.

Theo stands behind me. "Baby, you're already so drenched."

His fingers slide between my legs. I tense at the touch, but immediately miss it when he pulls it away. He grips my ass with both hands. He pulls one of his hands away and brings it down swiftly. My body tenses at the impact, but the pain burns so sweet. He gently massages the site of impact before repeating the motion. Just like the last time I received punishment, the second spanking is harder. I let out a soft moan as the pain lingers across my skin.

Theo slides his fingers through my arousal again, coating them while sliding inside me. I buck at the sensation, practically begging for more.

"Such a needy brat. If you had come home sooner, you could be cumming all over my cock by now." I roll my hips, hoping to create any friction, but he removes his fingers, leaving me empty. His fingers make their way to my clit, pressing gentle circles. His free hand slides up the back of my neck, gripping my hair and pulling it. He lifts my head off the bed while increasing the pace of his other fingers. My core tightens, but am left disappointed when he backs off. Depriving me of orgasms seems to be one of Theo's favorite hobbies.

"Theo," I groan.

"You made me wait. Now you must wait." He smacks my ass a third time before walking back to the couch. He picks something up off the couch before walking back to me. Something cold and smooth is placed against my pussy. Gently, Theo presses it into me. I moan as it fills me. Once Theo has it all the way in, I can also feel something pressed against my clit. Just as I am getting used to the new sensations, it begins to buzz. He put a vibrator inside me. The front portion comes to life and immediately starts to pulse on my clit. I gasp as my core begins to clench around the vibrator.

Theo watches for a minute as I begin to buck against the vibrator. It feels so good, but I can't get it to the exact spot I need.

I arch my back as the vibrator has been pressed against my G-spot. I gasp as my core tightens and lightning shoots through me.

"Good girl. You're so pretty when you cum," Theo says softly near my head. I have become so focused on what I was feeling in my body, I had forgotten about Theo. He walks back down the side of the bed and places himself behind me again. I am expecting to be spanked again, but when his hands touch me, he is being so gentle. He grips and massages my ass again, before reaching his hand into his pocket and pulling something out. The vibrator is still inside me and still pressing against my clit. The original wave subsided, but the pressure is building faster.

"Deep breaths, baby. You can take it." I try to do as I am told, but I can only manage some stuttered breaths.

As I breathe, something warm and wet has made its way to my ass. Theo has put lube on my asshole and is now gently pressing in with his thumb.

"Relax, Aria." He presses a little further, and I can feel myself stretch around him. "Good girl."

He uses his other hand to adjust the vibrator, and everything clenches as he places it back on just the right spots. He holds it in place with his knee, while he returns his hand to my lower back as he fingers my ass.

The pressure in my core continues to build. I pull on my restraints as my core pulses before waves of orgasm overtake me.

"You're being too quiet, baby. I thought my little brat wanted to play." A low chuckle rumbles through his chest.

"Theo. Please..."I beg as my breath hitches.

Theo gently removes his thumb, and I instantly miss his touch.

"Say it again, and say it right." He pulls away, leaving me missing how he felt all over my body.

"*Daddy*, please. I'm sorry," I plead in shuddering breaths. "Please."

Seconds later, I realize he places a cold, metal plug up against my ass before slowly pressing it in. It is larger than his thumb, and I can feel myself stretch even more to fit it, but once it's in, I feel myself approaching orgasm again.

My entire body tenses when I feel Theo bending over me. His warm breath against my neck.

"Give me another one. I want to hear you scream my name while you cum."

I pull hard on the restraints as I am flooded with release. Theo removes the vibrator, and my body slumps into the sheets. My body is spent.

Theo backs off of me. The cold air brushes over my skin, goosebumps rising everywhere he once touched.

"How are you doing, baby?" Theo asks from the couch.

"Mhmm," I murmured.

"Think you can continue?" I hear the sound of Theo's belt sliding out of his belt loops.

"Please, Daddy," I almost beg. Having had a minute to breathe without the vibrator inside me, I need more. I want to see how far we can take this. I want to feel everything Theo does to me tonight and tomorrow.

"God, you're perfect."

He walks closer to me and gently caresses the tops of my thighs. "Did you learn anything today, Aria?"

"If I don't listen, I get repeated orgasms?" I smile, knowing that is not the answer he wants to hear.

The snap of the leather against the back of my thighs stings. My entire body tenses, but after the initial sting begins to wear off, warmth fills my core.

"Do you want to try that again, Aria?"

"The answer or the slap?"

"The slap."

"Yes, please, Daddy." The backs of my thighs, still burning from the last slap, are hit again with the sharp slap that was even harder than the first. He is easing me in. I take a deep breath and exhale through my teeth. A dull throb begins to form where the belt made contact.

"Is that what you wanted, baby girl?"

"Yes, Daddy."

"Did you learn anything today?" he asks again. I'm tempted to tease him again, but I don't know if I can handle another slap of the belt.

I swallow hard before giving him my answer. "Not to make you wait."

"Good girl." Theo gently rubs an ice cube across the burning skin. I whimper at the contrast.

As it melts, he slowly traces it inside my thigh to my clit. He rubs circles with it until it fully melts. He keeps circling my clit as he pushes the vibrator back inside. Theo turns it on to a gentle setting, making it buzz both on my clit and inside of me before he places his cock at my entrance that is already full.

"Daddy," I whine.

"Do you want this, baby?"

"Yes." He slowly slides his cock, stretching me more than I have ever been. The pain is nothing compared to other parts of tonight, but the way my walls spasm around him and the vibrator is only seconds before I am seeing stars. I dissolve into pleasure as Theo finds his release.

All the toys are gently removed, my wrists and ankles are unbound, and Theo wraps me in a blanket on his bed. We lay there for a while catching our breath when Theo finally broke the silence.

"Give me a color, Aria."

"Green." I smile.

He kisses the top of my head. "That's my girl."

CHAPTER
Thirteen

THEO

I lean against the doorway, watching Aria type on her computer. Even though she is working from home, she was still up at eight a.m., starting on this project. I'd like to say that if I had known she wasn't going to sleep in today, I wouldn't have kept her so late last night. But that is not true. I didn't watch the clock at all last night, and don't plan on watching it anytime we are together in the future.

Last night was as perfect as I could have ever hoped. Watching her body react to everything I was doing, feeling her pussy clench around my cock as she came harder than I have ever seen from her. I asked a lot of her last night, and she gave it all without hesitation.

She looks up from her computer screen and sees me. Her face melts into a soft smile. I walk closer as she slides the laptop onto the table and gets to her knees to lean against the back of the couch.

Brushing a piece of hair out of her face, I cup her chin and lift it, bringing my lips down to her forehead.

"Hey, baby, sleep well?" I ask. Her eyes closed gently as I kneel down to be on her level. Her head nods gently against my hand.

"Are you doing ok today?" I fucked up yesterday and got ahead of myself. While we did talk about hard limits and safe words, we never discussed aftercare. This wasn't the first time we fucked, and I had an idea of what she likes after sex, but last night was intense, and while she didn't complain, I need to do better.

"Mhmm." She is still quiet.

I walk around and sit down on the couch, pulling Aria into my body. She snuggles in under my arm and pulls the laptop back into her lap, and opens her emails. I watch as she responds to a few from what I assume are other interns. But then a new email pops up as a notification at the top of her screen.

Luxury living in the city: Thank you for your application

She applied for an apartment? When? This morning? Did I push her too far? We discussed hard limits. I checked in, and she never pulled the safe word.

Did I ask too much?

Did I miss a sign?

Why wouldn't she have told me?

My body tenses as the rush of questions float through my head. She must notice, she looks over her shoulder at me.

Her confusion evident. I pull my arm away and stand up. My fingers run through my hair as I try to replay every check-in. *Did I not hear her correctly? Did she say something I missed?* She didn't pull away during after care.

I start pacing behind the couch. My body needs to find a release from all the anger now flooding my veins. How could I be so reckless? How could I hurt her on the first night I really had her?

Did she think it was aftercare for her, or was she giving me more of what she thought I wanted? I have tried to make her feel so safe, but why did she not feel safe enough to tell me to stop? I plant my hands on the kitchen counter and drop my head before picking up and throwing a glass at the marble backsplash.

Aria is intently watching my every move. She's folding in on herself. I saw this happen the other night. When she realized she had been roofied and didn't know what had happened. She was scared and started to shut down, and now she is doing the same exact thing. Except this time, it's my fault. I pushed her too far last night, and now I'm scaring her. Bile rises in my throat. I did this.

"I'm sorry." I'm not trying to scare her. I want to protect her, but I didn't protect her from myself.

"Daddy?" Her voice trembles the slightest bit.

"I'm sorry. I am not angry with you, baby. I am so sorry," I plead.

"What happened?"

"When are you moving?" I ask, defeated. I don't want to lose her, but I'm not going to force her to stay somewhere she doesn't feel comfortable.

"Moving? Do you want me to?" Her shoulders drop, her tone heartbroken. She pulls my full attention.

"No." I shake my head. "Never." I walk over to her and kneel down, putting my face below hers. *She doesn't want to move?*

"Why did you apply for an apartment if you weren't

planning on moving?" My gaze flicks back and forth between both her eyes.

"While you were gone, I was scared that when you came back, you would have changed your mind. Or that you will in a few weeks or months. I wanted to see what I could qualify for on my own so that when you do want me to leave, I'm not starting from nothing." She hides her face behind her hands.

"Baby..." I coax gently to get her to look at me. I place my hands on her legs, grateful for any contact. "I will not change my mind. If you ever want to leave, I will do everything in my power to set you up so you won't have to worry. But I will never ask you to leave." She lets a single tear fall. I slide my thumb across her cheek, wiping it away.

"I am sorry if I have not made that clear." She nods. "Next time you have any type of concern about us, come to me. Talk to me." She nods again.

I walk back and sit down on the couch, pulling her against me.

"Was the thought of me moving what made you so angry? I didn't mean to, I'm sorry." Aria begins to curl in on herself again. She is so scared of doing something wrong. She doesn't want to give me any excuse to push her away. I need to be careful with her right now. While she may say *green*, I need to be the one to make sure I'm not pushing too far. It's not consent if she is only doing it because she is scared of what would happen if she says no.

"Yes, but it's not your fault. I got so angry for letting myself push you too far, or missed signs that you needed something from me that you didn't get." Taking a deep breath, I continue. "I thought I hurt you, and that was why you were pulling away and leaving. I was mad at myself for not protecting you."

"You didn't do anything I didn't consent to. I never pulled red."

"Did you want to?" Bracing myself for the answer, my hands tense, gripping the loose fabric at her waist.

"No." Her voice is full of conviction. She is now consoling me. I pull her onto my lap so she is straddling me. She wraps her arms around my shoulders and nuzzles her face into my shoulder. We stay like this for a few minutes, just holding each other. She sits up and looks at me before apologizing again.

"Baby, there is no need to apologize. Just don't do that again, or you will need to earn my forgiveness." She smiles as I taunt her.

I didn't hurt her. I didn't push too far. She still wants to be here. She still wants me.

My phone buzzes, and I look down to see Enzo's desk number.

"Yes?"

"Mr. Reeves, there is a furniture delivery here for Ms. Mason. Can I send them up?"

"Yes. Thank you." I hang up the phone and look at Aria. "You have a delivery." She smiles and tries to get up. I pull her hips back down hard onto my lap. Her eyes widen as she realizes she is pressing herself against my very erect cock. Her gaze shoots down, then back to me.

"We don't have time to handle this right now, but we will as soon as these delivery people are gone." She bites her lip as she lets herself sink down a little further onto my body. I let out a soft groan as she starts rocking her hips against me.

"Aria," I warn.

"Daddy," she says sweetly as she does it again.

"Aria, that's two."

"And that's three," she whispers as her hips press against my cock and her lips press a kiss just behind my ear.

A loud knock at the door startles her. I pull her body against mine and stand up. She wraps her legs around my hips and her arms around my shoulders. I walk to the door and open it with one hand.

"Hi, make this quick."

"Where would you like this?" one of the men asks as they bring the box inside. Aria is giggling against my neck as I tell them to take it to the loft.

I place her down on the kitchen counter, but she doesn't loosen her grip on me.

"You are in so much trouble," I whisper into her hair.

"Good." She laughs.

"You don't need to put it together. Just put it upstairs and I'll handle the rest," I shout up the stairs.

As the men walk down the stairs, I unhook Aria from my body and leave her sitting on the counter. I grab my wallet and pull out a few $100 bills. As the delivery men walk by, I hand them the bills and lead them to the door. The second they are gone and the door is locked, I turn to Aria, who is sitting on the counter, so pleased with herself.

"How many was it?"

"Three."

"Three it is."

CHAPTER

Fourteen

ARIA

My body is wrapped around Theo as he carries me to his room. My chest tightens as we enter. Did I push this too far? Last night was intense, and I don't think I am ready to participate in anything like that again.

I slowly slide down Theo's body until my feet hit the floor. I look up to see Theo looking down at me. He is still the playful man who was in the living room with me. He hasn't become the disciplinarian he was last night.

While he may still *punish me*, it's in a more light-hearted way. I take a breath, knowing this is going to be fun.

"Strip." His only word breaking the silence.

"I mean, I could." I smile, taking a step back from him. His hand immediately grabs me by the throat and pulls me in. His fingers place gentle pressure on the sides of my neck, but aren't squeezing. I drop my head and smile up at him.

"Do you want to try that again, baby?" His voice is low.

"I think you should do it." I swallow, "I mean, a man takes what he wants, right?" Theo rolls his eyes and takes his free hand to lower my shorts. Once they slide down to my ankles, I help him out and step out of them.

"Your sass is going to get you in trouble today."

"Good." I like to press these buttons. I like seeing the way his jaw tightens or how he swallows hard when I push back. His grip releases my throat as he lifts the hem of the shirt I stole from his closet last night, pulling it over my head. I clench my thighs as my body already begins to react. Just the way this man looks at me has me wanting to feel him inside me.

Theo's gaze travels down my body before stepping back.

"Are you going to be a good girl today?" I nod my head. Anything he wants, I want to feel his dick twitch inside me as he cums. I want to have his hands all over my body. I want to do whatever he wants so I can get what I need. I nod my head.

"On your knees." I immediately do as he says. My mouth begins to water as I start anticipating tasting him, feeling him in the back of my throat. Knowing the way his muscles tense and contract is because of me. I look up at him, begging him to continue.

Let me touch you.

"Pull it out." My hands instantly pull at his waistband, freeing his cock. My hand wraps around him, and I bite my lip. He hasn't given me permission yet. As much as I just want to take it and be punished afterward, I know he will punish me by not giving me what I want.

"My little slut is becoming such a good listener." He brushes my hair behind my ear. "Open up, make me cum, baby."

I lift him slightly so I can place my tongue at the base of his shaft and lick to his tip. I flick my tongue against the sensitive spot on the bottom before taking his tip into my mouth. I gently suck the tip, running my hand up and down his length.

Theo lets out a soft gasp as I take him fully into my mouth. I take him until I feel him hit the back of my throat, bouncing my head up and down a few times, coating his dick in my spit, using it as lube. I twist my wrist while I continue to stroke his shaft.

He lets out a pleased groan, and that's all the encouragement I need to continue.

"Aria." His voice commanding but still soft. I look at him, slowly pulling my mouth to his tip.

"Don't stop, but use this to make yourself cum." He drops the vibrator he used on me last night. I swallow hard as my core already tightens. I pick it up slowly and find the power button, turning it on and picking the setting.

I take him in deep as I slowly place the vibrating silicone inside me. I can't keep myself from moaning around Theo's dick as I press it against my clit. I take his dick deep and swallow hard around the tip. His fingers lace in my hair on the back of my head.

Yes, Daddy, please take control.

He holds me in place, pushing himself deeper. "Perfect," he praises as he begins to thrust. Tears well in my eyes, but I don't want this to stop. I want this, I want him. I press my legs tighter together as waves of pleasure roll through my core. I buck my hips, wanting every last bit of orgasm.

"Good girl," Theo growls as he thrusts one last time, hard and deep, holding himself in the back of my throat. My entire body tenses as I can't hold off the shockwaves taking over my body. I choke out a sob around Theo's cock, pushing him to his orgasm, sending warm ropes of cum down the back of my throat.

I suck hard on his cock as he slowly pulls out, making sure I take every drop he gives me. I swallow hard and try to catch my breath. Theo leans down, putting us eye to eye.

"That was one. On the bed, baby girl."

Fuck, there's going to be three of these.

I teased him three times. My body is still recovering from the first one as he helps me to my feet and then guides me back to the bed. "On your back." I climb onto the bed and lie back, but he pulls me to the edge, pushing my legs open. He kneels to the ground, and the sight of him as he places his lips on my inner thigh has me about to cum, but I know he won't let me off that easily. He slowly kisses closer to my center, taking his time. His warm breath against my clit has my body tensing. Still sensitive from my first orgasm, my breath stutters.

"You taste so good, baby." He grips my thighs tighter as he slides his tongue up my wetness. "So good."

"Theo," I breathe. He immediately stops. He pulls back.

"Try that again, Aria."

"Daddy," I moan. He immediately puts his tongue back on me, circling my clit. My hips jerk as the pressure builds, but Theo places one of his arms over my hips, holding me down.

"Daddy," I whine. I don't know how much longer I can hold this one off.

"Not yet, I'm not done." He slides his fingers inside me before returning his mouth to my clit.

He sucks on my clit hard. His grip on my hips tightens as I can't keep myself from riding his face. Pulling my clit between his teeth, he bites gently. Not enough to cause pain, but enough to set fireworks off throughout my body. He pulls away, with a smug smile and a wet chin.

"That's two."

Theo stands and climbs onto the bed, leaning himself against the headboard. "Come here, baby." He stretches out a hand. I roll over and crawl next to him. He pulls me against his body, letting me rest my head on his chest for just a brief moment.

"You're not done yet." He smiles. "How many did I say?"

"Three," I whisper.

"Three."

He pulls me up so I am straddling his lap. He isn't even inside me, but heat pools in my core, feeling his dick against me.

I shift my weight and inadvertently rub myself against Theo's cock. His fingers dig into my hips as he drops his head back. He is just as wound up as I am. This may actually be fun, a little payback. I smile, repeating the motion.

"Take what you need, baby girl," he instructs as he adjusts his grip on my body. I slowly put my hand between us and grab his dick. I gently place him at my entrance before lowering myself onto him. I grab onto the headboard for balance, slowly rolling my hips. Theo licks his thumb before placing it against my clit. I gasp as the pressure in my core intensifies.

I keep taking his cock as deep as I can get him, thrusting slowly. He lifts his chest and pulls me lower. His lips make contact with my nipple, gently pulling it into his mouth. I start to lose my rhythm as his tongue swirls. Theo grips my waist tighter, stopping me. He lifts me slightly while dropping his hips. Lowering himself, my core tightens, already missing the feeling of him. He thrusts deep and hard. He continues this pace while also sucking harder.

He lets go of my nipple to kiss the side of my breast. He buries himself in me as he sinks his teeth into my skin.

I let out an almost scream. Theo releases me.

"Color?" he checks in.

"Green," I pant. He thrusts harder while pulling my nipple back between his teeth. I slide my knees further apart, letting myself sink down on him even further.

The fire in my gut rises as his fingers dig into my ass cheek in a way that is gently grazing my asshole. My breath hitches remembering the feeling of being so full. He doesn't ask with his words, but I want it. I need it.

"Green," I breathe out. "Please." He presses his finger against my hole, pushing in. I tense at the intrusion, but it feels so good. He bucks his hips as his teeth clamp down on my nipple. The pain sends electricity through my veins.

My entire body tenses as the walls of my pussy strangle his cock. He places his tongue against my nipple, soothing the sting as he holds himself deep inside me. His cock twitches, filling me with his release.

"Three," I whisper, my body exhausted. Theo pulls me to him, wrapping his arms around my body, holding me to his chest.

"You did so well, baby. You take me so well." He pushes the hair out of my face, kissing my forehead as I fall asleep.

CHAPTER
Fifteen

THEO

TWO MONTHS LATER

I look down at my watch; it's been twenty-five minutes. Aria usually takes thirty minutes in the shower when doing her aftercare routine. If she is going to have a warm towel when she gets out, I need to throw it in the dryer now. I head into the closet and pull one of the pink, plush bath towels off the shelf and toss it in the dryer. I should have just enough time to grab her drink from the kitchen and one of the Ferrero Rocher I had delivered. I had to have Enzo procure some after seeing how sad she was when she realized we didn't have any more. Working the magic he always does, a large box of little chocolate candies was delivered to my door.

As I make it upstairs, I hear the water turn off in the shower. *Fuck, she's done early.* I grab the towel from the dryer, throw her robe in, and walk it over to the glass shower entrance. I hand her her towel and love the sound of the soft moan she lets out when she feels the warmth snuggled around her hands.

"Your drink is on the counter." I kiss the top of her head, and she wraps herself in the towel. I swear, if you had told me a few months ago that not only would I meet someone and feel comfortable enough to bring her home, but she would live with me and have hot pink and blue things strewn all over my house, I would have thought you were crazy. But seeing how happy it all makes Aria has definitely made them some of my favorite things I have ever purchased. Once she's wrapped up, I pull her into a hug, resting my chin on the top of her head.

"Anything else I can get you?"

"I wish we had candy," she says, laying her wet hair on my chest.

"Look on the counter." Her eyes shoot to where her cup is, and I can see the moment her eyes find the little gold wrapper.

"How did you—" she asks with the biggest smile on her face.

"If a golden chocolate is part of your aftercare, I will always have golden chocolate for aftercare. Now get dressed so you can pick what we're going to watch." I smack her ass as she walks into the closet. I lean against the counter as I wipe away the water she left on my chest. Tossing the towel onto the counter, I can't help but just relax into our new normal. We have found a rhythm and routine. She has integrated herself into my life so well. It helps that the Court has been fairly quiet, not needing to pull me away on anything. I will have to figure out how to let her in on that part of my life somehow, but for now, I am just focusing on keeping us happy.

Aria walks out of the closet in a pair of black shorts and a crop top, letting me see all the places that marks from this morning are forming. I trace the line on her thigh where a bruise is starting to show.

Noticing where my attention is, she leans forward onto the counter, giving me a full view of several marks beginning to show below and on her ass. My hands grip her hips and pull her back into me, leaning down so my chest is touching her back. I rake my teeth down her neck, gently sinking them into her shoulder. She arches back into me at the pain.

"Such a good girl," I whisper as I kiss where my teeth just left imprints in her skin, then up her neck. "Let's go." Pulling away from her, I head into the closet and pull her robe from the dryer. I hand it to her, then head out to the living room to turn on the TV. I make it most of the way until I hear banging on my front door. I pull out my phone to see missed calls from Enzo. *This can't be good.*

Right after the knocks, I can hear muffled shouting from the foyer. Sounds like security is shouting at somebody who is not supposed to be here. Aria makes her way to the living room, hearing the commotion.

"What's going on?" There's a tremble in her voice that I have heard before. I quickly walk to her side and help her finish wrapping herself in the plush robe.

"It's nothing," I try to reassure. "Security is outside handling it. Let's get you comfortable, and then I will go check on what's going on." She listens, but isn't convinced. How the fuck somebody was able to get all the way up to the penthouse doors without permission is inexcusable. Enzo did call, but I need to know who fucked up and let this happen.

Aria sits in her spot on the couch, and I make my way to

the door. I am able to start making out some of the things being said.

"You don't belong here!"

"You need to leave."

"I have every right to be here!" a female voice that almost sounds familiar screams.

"Ma'am, you are trespassing."

It's a woman. What woman would be ballsy enough to show up at my door? I swing the door open, knowing the odds are in my favor if this gets physical.

Once I see who is standing in front of me, I freeze.

One of the security guards immediately begins to apologize.

"We are so sorry for the inconvenience, Mr. Reeves. She snuck into the stairwell after we told her you weren't allowing guests," he quickly rattles off. I just raise my hand, telling him to stop. I don't want excuses right now.

Right now, the only thing I need to know is why my ex-fiancée is standing in my doorway.

"Alana?" I ask.

"Where is she?" she shouts.

"That's none of your business." My arms cross across my chest. She is unwelcome, but not a danger.

"She's my daughter." I can't help but laugh. They may be biologically related, but that woman was never a mother to Aria.

"She is an adult."

"Where is she?"

"Why do you care?"

We shout back and forth at each other until the only voice I care about interrupts.

"Mom?"

CHAPTER
Sixteen

ARIA

"What the fuck are you doing here?"

"I needed to see you." She tries to play the concerned parent, a role she never quite mastered.

"And being told we didn't want to see you wasn't a clear enough message?" Of course, it didn't. She does whatever she wants.

"I—I—"

"Stop. We don't want you here." Theo stands behind me, my back against his ribs. I am so grateful he is here for this, and I am not having to do this alone. My hand finds his, and he squeezes gently without his attention leaving my mom.

"Aria," she pleads softly, "let me take you home. We can start over and pretend this never happened?"

"And why the fuck would she want to do that?" Theo barks from behind me. My body jerks in surprise, but his free hand grips my hip. His thumb caresses my side, a protective measure letting me know he is still here for me. That he may be angry, but not with me.

"This doesn't involve you," she snaps at Theo.

"Why would I want to forget this ever happened?" I repeat Theo's question. I really want to know how she spun this in her head. How what she's proposing makes any sense.

"I mean, I wouldn't want to remember months where I was kidnapped, held hostage, used, and manipulated." Somehow, even when she is calling me a victim, she can't hide the judgment in her voice. If what she was saying was true, she would blame me for it and would twist it and use it to belittle me. Like, somehow being kidnapped and tortured was all my fault, completely inconveniencing her.

Theo's grip tightens on me at the accusation. His fingers press so deeply into my skin that I know I will have perfectly round bruises clustered on my hip later.

"What are you even talking about?"

"You disappeared, Aria." She almost sounds genuinely concerned. "You disappeared with a man who has a track record of abandoning women once he had his fill."

"That's not what happened, and you know it." Now I am getting proactive over Theo. I will not let her spin things. She is not the victim here.

"Why else would he have left? We were perfect together!" she screams at Theo. It has been over twenty years, and she still hasn't figured out that, like almost everything that goes wrong in her life, their relationship ended because of her poor choices.

"How about the fact you were fucking my best friend?" Theo grits through his teeth. I can feel the heat radiating off of him. This time, I am the one squeezing his hand. She isn't worth it.

"You knew that wasn't serious." Theo pulls me a step back as my mother tries to move closer.

"Serious enough that you married and had a kid with him." The words shouted are full of disgust.

"Only because you left. You left me to raise a child by myself!"

"A child that wasn't mine!" His voice booms over my head.

"The child that you're speaking of is standing right here." I push Theo's hand off of me and step away. He tenses as I pull away. He tries to reach out for my hand, but I pull my hands into the sleeves of my robe before crossing my arms. I just need a minute. I am not sure if I should be happy he has been able to fully separate the idea of me being the daughter of his ex, or disgusted about the way he is referring to my existence right now.

She takes this moment to move closer to me, thinking maybe her argument is working.

"Aria, come home with me. I just want to protect you." She tries to place her hand on my shoulder, but I shrug her off.

"Protect me? From what?" What does she think she can protect me from now? Now that I'm an adult and can protect myself. Where was this urge to protect me when I was constantly bullied, harassed, or shunned because of her lies?

"Him." She shoots a glare over her shoulder at Theo.

"Him? Why would you need to protect me from him?" I laugh. Theo was distraught when he thought he had pushed me too far. He could never intentionally hurt me.

"Aria, when you disappeared—"

"Left. I didn't disappear, I *left*. I chose to leave." I will correct her every time.

"When you *left*, the police wouldn't help me find you. Said you were an adult and you were allowed to move."

"Which is absolutely correct," Theo interjects.

"So when the police wouldn't help me, I got in touch with a private investigator. I told him I was worried about you and that Theo had threatened you, which is why you left."

"I left to get away from you." I don't understand how she can't wrap her head around that fact.

"Well, he looked into the man you trust so much." Here it is, what lie has she cooked up this time? "He confirmed a lot of my suspicions. Aria. Theo is dangerous." Theo's body tenses.

Everyone has used the word powerful, when describing Theo. No one has said he was dangerous.

"What are you even talking about?" She needs to just tell us the lie so we can move on.

"Theo is working with the mafia." Her voice is filled with conviction. She honestly believes this shit. I look at Theo, expecting to share a laugh, but his gaze is fixed on the front door, jaw tight and unmoving. "He is either going to leave you because of his job, or put you in serious danger because of it."

This shit can't be real. I look back at my mom, who is still talking.

"When he left me, he got mixed up with this really sketchy group of guys. People he met at Acadia." *Theo went to Acadia University?* I guess that makes sense, so many of his friends are alumni, as well. "And the PI talked to some of your new coworkers. He was told that they have seen you with Theo. That he uses intimidation to control and manipulate you. They have also noticed several bruises. They said you never explain how you got them and brush it off."

Her eyes flick down to where my robe has fallen off my shoulder. Theo's bite mark is now showing.

"You don't have to let him hurt you anymore."

"He doesn't!" I shout as I fix my sleeve and tie the robe around myself tighter.

He doesn't manipulate me. He has never coerced me into doing something I didn't want. He would never hurt me, and there is a difference between being intimidated and someone using intimidation. Jonathan is just intimidated. He has expressed his concern before; he has to be the one talking to the PI.

"He frequents Acadia; he was just there a couple of weeks ago. He must have gotten you in his sights and then strategically placed himself in your life. He is manipulating you. He stalked you, and now is abusing you."

I look to Theo for answers. His face just dropped to the floor.

"Theo?"

He finally looks at me.

"Were you at Acadia that weekend you left?"

"Yes."

"Did you meet me at Acadia? "

"No."

"He's lying!" My mom's voice rings in my ear. "He won't tell you the truth, bab—"

"Don't call me that!" I cut her off. I don't want to hear her try to use a sweet term of endearment when lying to me, especially not one that Theo uses.

The little voice at the back of my head telling me he is keeping secrets, that I'm not getting the entire story, keeps getting louder and louder.

He is lying. He is keeping secrets. He doesn't trust you. He is going to leave. He doesn't love you. You're dispensable. You're temporary.

The words repeat over and over, increasing in volume until I can barely hear the shouting match happening between Theo and my mom.

"You stalked her!"

"I did not!"

"You are hurting her!"

"The only one hurting her here is you. You have done nothing but torture her for your mistakes the entire time she lived in your home!"

"You're just using her to get back at me! Was this your plan? Play the long game? Use my daughter to punish me for an honest mistake?"

"Honest mistake? You fucked half the town, the only mistake here is you."

"What are you going to do when you get bored with her? Up and leave? Leave her with nothing? No goodbye, no answer? That seems to be your MO. How long until you get bored with her? When you get her pregnant? Going to abandon her then? How long until she is all used up? You know she got passed around quite a bit already, I bet she can't even tell you how many men she's fucked!"

"Do not talk about her that way! She is your daughter, not you. You have no right to judge what she did with her body. The only reason you were judged is because you were in a committed relationship, you ruined lives!"

"Whose life did I ruin? You seem to have done just fine!"

"Aria's!"

How much of what she is saying is true? Where does he work? What does he do? Why is he always back at Acadia? Did he really meet me while I was there? Is he going to leave? Am I not enough? I know I can't trust my mom, but Theo isn't denying some of these things. Can I trust him?

The questions race through my head. Pressure builds in my chest, making it hard to breathe. I try to catch my breath, but I can't. I can't get a deep breath no matter how hard I try. The room begins to spin.

"Red."

CHAPTER
Seventeen

ARIA

Red. Red. Red.

I need the thoughts to stop. I need the voices quieted. I need the shouting to end.

"Daddy." My voice soft, but it's all I can muster. "Red."

Theo stops mid-sentence and immediately puts all his focus on me.

My hands gripped tightly together at my chest. Our eyes meet as a tear slides down my cheek.

"Get her out of here," he shouts to security, who has had a front row seat to my family drama. "If she puts up a fight, call the cops. Have her arrested for trespassing and assault. Maybe she will add resisting arrest and do us all a favor." His eyes never leave mine.

The door slams behind him. He slowly walks over to me.

"Aria." His voice is gentle. "How can I help?" His blue eyes soften as he reaches out and places his hands on my shoulders.

"I-It's too much." My voice hitches mid-sentence. My

lungs still won't let me breathe. My short and shallow breaths are the only thing keeping me from passing out, but that doesn't seem too far away.

Theo places his hands on either side of my face, keeping my eyes locked on his.

"Aria, I need you to listen to me and me alone." His voice commanding, like when he is instructing me in the bedroom. These are words he expects to be obeyed. I focus on trying to only hear his voice. I close my eyes, trying to get the warring thoughts inside my head to quiet.

"Eye contact. You will look at me." My eyes snap open and find his eyes unwavering, just staring into mine. I flick back and forth between his eyes as he starts giving me more instructions. My hands begin to tremble, and Theo gently lowers his to wrap around my fists.

"Try to take a deep breath. In for four, out for four."

In—One. Two. Three. Four.

Out—One. Two. Three. Four.

The numbers chant inside my head. Theo takes deep breaths with me, leading by example.

"Again."

We continue this pattern until I can take an uninterrupted breath. My lungs have opened, and I am no longer inching closer to passing out.

My hands stop shaking.

"What do you need, baby?"

My eyes drop to my hands. "I-I don't know." I close my eyes and drop my head.

"Can you tell me what happened?" He doesn't force me to look at him. He isn't commanding me to tell him. He is asking.

"There were things you didn't deny," I whisper. "I want to trust you, but—"

The accusations my mother made they can't be true. I am sure some things lined up, but if you draw enough lines anywhere, they will eventually form a picture. The thoughts begin to gain traction again.

He's lying. You can't trust him. What if your mom is right?

My breaths start to get shorter. The air around me gets thicker.

"What can I do?"

"I nee-need the thoughts to stop. I need to know I can trust you," I practically beg. Another tear falls from my eye.

Theo pulls me into his chest, placing one arm around my back and his other hand cradling my neck. I can feel the rise and fall of his chest as he holds me against him.

"Come here, I have an idea." He lifts me into his arms. I wrap my arms over his shoulders and my legs around his waist, a position we find ourselves in often. The familiarity is comforting, but the worry that I can't trust him doesn't settle.

He leads us to his room. He closes the door behind him, something he doesn't do often. When the only people in the house are us, there isn't really a need for privacy. He wants to shut out everything but right here and right now, with him. There is nothing beyond that door worth a second thought right now.

He sits me on the side of the bed. Kneeling before me, he slides my robe off.

"I want to help you turn those thoughts off. Is that ok?"

I want them off. I want it all to stop. I want Theo to take control and put me in a space where the only thing I hear is him.

I only nod, giving him permission.

"Lay back, hands up." I slide further into the bed and do as I am told. I watch as Theo pulls a set of soft restraints from the bedside table. Once he secures my wrists in the cuffs, he attaches the cuffs to the bedframe.

"Do you remember the first night I restrained you?" He walks to the couch at the end of the bed, giving him a perfect view of me.

"Yes." I immediately flash back to the night in Texas, when he used a tie to bind my hands.

"Tell me about it." He leans forward, putting his elbows on his knees. He isn't sitting back and watching. He is holding himself back, making sure he is giving me what I need.

"I had just had your cock in my mouth." I swallow. "You fucked my face until you came and then wanted to watch me touch myself." My core tightens at the memory, and all the times we have been in a similar position begin flashing through my mind. I swallow, trying to find words to describe it.

"Then?" he asks, encouraging me to continue.

"I did as I was told. You were watching me and I wanted to gi-give you a show, so I started playing with my nipple." Warmth rises in my core. He lifts his gaze to me, watching me again, but this time it's different. That time it was fun and new. This time, there's so much more behind it. "You told me to stop, or there would be consequences."

"Did you stop?"

"No. I pulled harder. So you took away my hands."

"And?"

"You used me how you wanted."

"Why did you let me do that?"

"I wanted it." I did, I wanted him to find his pleasure

however he wanted to with me. I wanted to be a tool for him to use.

"And you trusted me?"

"I did." Theo drops his head again at my wording.

"Do you still trust me?"

"Yes." The word comes out of my mouth before I could even think about it. Even with the worry and fears, my body knows I am safe with Theo.

He stands and walks to the head of the bed. I follow his movement as he pulls something else out of the nightstand. He dangles a black silk blindfold next to me.

"Still trust me?" I look from the blind fold to him, and nod my head. I take a deep breath as he gently places it over my eyes. In a moment, the room goes black. Nerves rise within me. I wiggle my wrists, testing the cuffs, proving they are secure.

"Deep breath," Theo instructs. I do as I am told, hoping it will calm the anxiety. It works momentarily, but now, not being able to see Theo and focus on the things around me, the thoughts I am trying to escape from grow louder.

He is using you. He doesn't care about you. He's going to leave you.

I hear a door open. I can't tell if it was the bedroom door or the closet door, but my heart begins to race.

"Theo," I whimper, begging for something to prove he is still there. But he doesn't answer. I try to take another deep breath, but it keeps getting caught in my throat.

I pull harder on the cuffs, but they still don't budge. My heart begins to beat out of my chest.

I try again, "Theo," this time louder. I can't hear any movement. I want to trust him, but this is becoming too much. He left. I am alone. I'm tied up and vulnerable, and he left me alone. I can't free myself. I can't protect myself. I'm helpless.

You're helpless, he left. He's going to do this over and over again, leaving you with nothing.

"Yellow." I hear things hit the floor as Theo walks closer to the bed.

CHAPTER
Eighteen

THEO

I turn so fast that everything that was on the end table crashes to the floor. I need to get to Aria. Standing to the side of her, I try to assess the situation. Aria is breathing heavier, and tears stream down her face. She has brought her knees up, making herself as small as she can.

"Baby." I place my hands on her, looking for anything that could be hurting her.

"Daddy, please," she begs.

"Please, what? What's going on, baby?" I brush her hair out of her face.

"Ple-please do-don't leave," she stutters. I wipe the tears from under her eyes and place my hands on either side of her face.

"I'm not going anywhere."

"I couldn't hear you." She swallows hard. I was too quiet from the couch. "I thought you were gone."

"I'm still here, baby, I'm not going anywhere." I use my thumb to wipe away a few of her tears. "I am so sorry I made you feel that way. Do you want to continue, or are you done?"

"No." I shake my head, confused.

"No, what?"

"I want to continue." I lean down and gently kiss her forehead.

"Thank you for trusting me. Thank you for letting me in to help you. You are truly amazing, Aria." I try to speak calmly and comfort her. She doesn't need dominance now; she needs care, and she's letting me be the one to provide it. "Even when your body is turning against you, you trust that when you pull the safe word, I am going to listen." Her breathing settles. "I am going to walk around the bed. It's just you and me, and I am not going anywhere."

I know that at the beginning of our relationship, she was very scared that I would leave. She did eventually trust me and was able to be vulnerable. Some of the accusations from her mom may have stirred up those fears of abandonment again. In a little while, we will have to sit and have those hard conversations. But for right now, I want Aria to take a break from the anxiety and only be able to think of the good. Because we are so good together.

"I'm right here." I place my hand on the top of her foot. "I need you to relax, okay?"

She nods her head before taking a deep breath.

"Do you remember that night you missed check-in?" I ask softly.

"Yes."

"How, when I told you to grab specific things, you did it?" She nods. Her breathing has calmed down, but it still stutters from time to time. "Why did you listen?"

"Because you asked."

"You did do as you were told, but why did you decide to listen? Why didn't you push back?"

She takes a deep breath before responding, "I trusted you."

"What made you trust me?"

"You hadn't hurt me before." I trace my fingers over a healing bite mark on her hip.

"But now I have." Did we move too fast? She has pulled colors before, and we always check in and adjust. Does she think because of how rough we play, I will hurt her intentionally?

"No," she quickly argues. "I mean, you have, but never in a way I didn't want."

Her breath hitches as I slide my fingers up her chest.

"So you trust me to not hurt you."

"Yes, you have never pushed me past what I said was ok."

"You now understand that even though you're scared, you trust me to have your best interest at heart?"

"Yes, Daddy." I open the nightstand drawer and pull out the vibrator I know Aria prefers. I sit next to her on the bed and turn it on. It begins to buzz, and Aria immediately picks up on the sound.

I gently place it on her chest, dragging it slowly between her breasts, laying it on her chest as I grab the pair of nipple clamps off the nightstand. The crop top she is wearing barely covers her tits as it is. I barely had to lift it to expose her nipples. I clip them on. She arches her back, taking in the new sensation.

I pick the vibrator back up and continue to drag it down her body. I lay it on her stomach, letting her feel the vibration in her core as I slide her shorts down to her knees. I could take them all the way off, but this also limits her motion. I slowly lift the vibrator from her stomach and continue to drag it painfully slow to her cunt. The moment it starts to slide between her legs, I freeze.

Her breaths quicken as she waits for me to put it where she needs.

"Please…" she breathes.

I lower it just enough, not quite on her clit, but close enough for her to feel some of the vibration. She lifts her hips, trying to get it that last little bit.

"Patience, baby." I rub her thigh. She takes a breath and relaxes her hips.

I then lower it to where she has been wanting it.

It doesn't take long to see it already starting to affect her.

She moans as her abs begin to tense.

She pulls at the restraints, trying to find leverage.

Her moans fill the room, my dick hardening with just the sound.

Right before Aria is about to cum, I turn it up.

"Breathe, baby, you can do this."

"No," she pants just before I can see her body at its peak.

"Theo!" she screams out as she cums. I turn the vibrator down, but not off.

"Good girl." I breathe against her neck.

I turn it up as I instruct, "Now give me another one."

CHAPTER
Nineteen

ARIA

"The water is warm, I'll go get your drink and snack." Theo begins to leave before I grab his hand.

"Daddy?" He turns around quickly. "Can you stay this time?"

"Absolutely." He pulls off his shirt, then his sweat pants, before picking me up off the counter and walking me into the shower. We stand under the spray of water for several minutes, just letting the warm water run down our bodies. When I finally decide it's time to get clean, Theo massages my head as he washes my hair.

"Thank you," I whisper, unsure if he even heard it.

"For what?"

"Everything?" What don't I have to thank him for? He protected me against my mother, he helped calm an anxiety attack, he put me in a position where I was able to see that no matter how loud my fears were, I trusted him, he proved himself trustworthy, he gave me multiple orgasms, and now he is being gentle and washing my hair. There are a lot of things to thank him for.

"You don't have to thank me for any of that. I just care about you and want to make sure you're ok." He pulls the handheld sprayer off the wall and begins rinsing my hair. "Are you ok?"

Rocks settle in the bottom of my stomach. "Honest answer?"

"Please."

"I don't know." I really don't. I mean, my mom made some wild accusations. If I were to believe her over Theo with some of the wildest lies she threw out today, it would show that I have absolutely zero trust in Theo and this relationship. But the way he responded to some of the things she said, and not denying the obvious lies, is worrisome. Why couldn't he just say they weren't true?

"Do you want to talk about it?" he asks while grabbing my conditioner and working it into my hair.

"Yeah, in a little. I don't think I'm quite ready to know just yet."

Theo runs his fingers up the back of my neck before grabbing a handful of my hair and pulling my head back. "You just like getting spoiled in the shower." Pressing his lips against mine, he smiles.

I smile as he pulls away. "You can't be mad when you're the one who made me a princess."

Theo grabs me a fresh towel, and while I'm drying off, he runs downstairs to get my drink and chocolate. When Theo said I could have whatever I wanted as aftercare, I probably should have gone bigger, like new shoes. But that little golden wrapped piece of heaven really does make me happy.

I throw on another pair of tiny athletic shorts and a clean

crop top. I love watching Theo get distracted, noting all the love marks he left on my body when I wear outfits like this.

I walk out of our room to the room next door. He has had me sleeping in his bed ever since he got home, but I still made this guest room my own. We usually are only in here for aftercare since Theo never put a TV in the main bedroom. Plus, we usually have to clean the sheets, and I don't want to have to delay my cuddles and trash TV to wrestle with a fitted sheet.

I climb into the bed and fix the pillows behind me. Theo walks in with my Dr. Pepper and chocolate, placing it gently on the nightstand before climbing into bed with me.

"So are we talking before or after we find out who cheated?"

"And you say you don't pay attention." I laugh. "It was Charlie and Liza."

"You watched ahead? I was guessing Buckley and Liza."

"No, I have social media." I turn the TV on and find our show, but don't hit play. "I guess we should talk first."

"If that is what you want to do."

"I don't want to do it at all, but this is something we can't ignore." Theo agrees, but he doesn't say anything.

I start to pick at my fingernails. After today, I am definitely going to have to schedule a spa day.

"Why couldn't you deny some of the things my mom accused you of?"

"Is that what got you so worked up, that I didn't deny the things she was saying?" Theo clarifies, but doesn't answer.

"Partially. There have been a lot of lingering feelings that have just gone unaddressed from the beginning, but hearing some outrageous claims being thrown at you, where would deny some but not all, was really confusing."

If he hadn't denied anything, that would be one thing, but he did deny some. He shot down some things that were absolutely false, but he didn't make it known that other things weren't true.

"I'm sorry I made this so confusing for you." While I appreciate the apology, he still hasn't actually answered. My anxiety begins to turn into anger. It's one thing to keep secrets, but skirting around the question and gaslighting me is an insult to my intelligence.

"How am I supposed to trust you when I know you're actively lying to me?" The words come out sharper than I intended, but I get my point across.

Theo looks away and stares at the TV for a minute, even though it's just displaying a static ad.

"Why did it seem like there was some truth in what my mom was saying when she said you were going to leave me, or put me in danger because of some secret mafia?"

"I won't leave you, Aria, and I will do everything in my power to keep you safe." Still not an answer, but at least we're closer to one. I think about his words. He is again not denying it; in a way, he is kind of confirming it. That my mom was lying about him leaving me because of his job, but not that his job would put me in danger.

"I'm still not getting complete answers, Theo. How am I supposed to be able to fully submit and trust when all I get are half-truths? Trust is earned, and I trust you not to hurt me, but I don't know if I can trust you with anything else. You have asked for so much blind trust *from* me, but you don't have any trust *in* me."

That last sentence seems to hit hard. I don't want to hurt him, but I also need to protect myself. I need to know what I'm up against if I am going to keep myself safe and be able to fully support Theo. If he is going to keep secrets from me for the entire time we're together, this isn't going to work.

"Aria, I need just a few more minutes of blind trust. I know I haven't earned it, but, baby, I promise this is the last time I will hide anything from you," Theo pleads.

My heart wants to trust, since that's what it has been doing for the last few months. My head argues that it won't be the last time; every time will be the *last time*. I can't keep doing this.

I find a compromise, I'll give him blind trust one last time, but if he keeps anything from me again, I'll leave. It will be hard, but I can't be somewhere where I'm not trusted.

"Fine, last time."

Before the words are fully out of my mouth, he is out of the bed, phone in hand, making a call. He kisses my forehead before leaving the room.

I really hope I didn't just make a huge mistake.

CHAPTER
Twenty

THEO

"I just need a guarantee she will be safe from us and because of us."

"If you are sure, you have it. But if she becomes a threat to The Court, we will have to take action."

"She won't."

"Then she is an extension of you and will be treated as such."

I end the call and take a deep breath before re-entering the bedroom. Aria is still sitting on the bed, TV paused, and just staring down at her hands in her lap.

"You're right."

Her face snaps up in my direction and waits for more information.

"There were things your mom said that I could not deny, and still be able to tell you I have never lied to you." Her gaze remains focused on me as I walk back into the room and onto my side of the bed. "You're also right that you deserve the truth. I have asked so much blind trust from you and given none in return."

I sit down on the foot of the bed, giving us space to talk. This is going to be a difficult conversation, and I want her to know I am here for her, but also give her space to process everything.

"I need you to know I wasn't hiding things from you because I don't trust you." I swallow hard. "I hid them because I am trying to protect you. But seeing how hurt you are because of the secrets, I can't keep them from you anymore."

I never made a plan for telling someone about my life and career. I never thought I would get close enough to anyone that not only would I want to tell them my secrets, but close enough that they were in danger from them. She deserves to know, and now that I know she will be protected, I have no reason to hide anything from her.

"I know you say you don't want secrets, but you have to understand these secrets will put your safety at risk. Are you sure you want to take that risk, to keep my secrets?"

Her gaze drops for a moment before looking straight into my eyes and nodding her head.

"Yes. I would rather know there's a risk and be told the truth, than things be hidden from me." Her voice not as confident as I think she is trying to sound, but she has made her decision.

"Let's get some of the accusations out of the way that were completely false: I didn't abandon Alana. I broke up with her, end of story." Aria nods. I really hoped this wasn't one she held onto, but with the chaos of the argument and her anxiety attack, even if I feel like the answer is obvious, it needs to be addressed. No room for doubt.

"I am not using you in any way to get back at your mom. I don't care about your past. I will not leave or abandon you, especially if you get pregnant." I am still not sure where she stands on kids, but whatever she decides, I will support her. Aria nods in understanding. She still hasn't spoken, and it's making me nervous.

"I am not intentionally trying to manipulate you in any way. It is a very real fear for me in our dynamic." Aria tilts her head at this.

"What do you mean?"

"I am fully aware that there is a power imbalance between us. I am settled in my well-paying career, and you are a new graduate, so between age, wealth, and social status, I have much more power than you do at this time. Not to mention, we are in a dynamic where you willingly give me more control. I never want to abuse that. I don't want you to feel pressured into anything you don't want to do because you feel like you have to for whatever reason. I am very aware that men in positions like mine abuse their standing, and I never want to do that to you, even unintentionally."

"But you like having control and power." Her lips lift into a soft smirk. A small bit of tightness releases from my chest, realizing that was never one of her fears.

"I like it given to me *willingly*, I don't like forcing it or taking it."

"What about Acadia?" she asks. *How could I forget her mother accused me of stalking her?*

"Yes, I frequent Acadia often, for my job. We recruit from there, and it is the usual meeting ground when I have business meetings. I was there a lot while you were a student. But I don't ever remember meeting you, and trust me, I would remember."

"There was no stalking or manipulation. You coming to Texas was a coincidence?"

"An inevitability. No matter how much I tried to move my mom out here, she was stubborn and would not leave. I was going to have to go back to my hometown eventually, and that is what happened."

"You said business meetings. You still haven't explained to me what your job is."

"Your mom was incorrect when she said I worked for the mafia." A brief sigh of relief leaves Aria, and my heart shatters, knowing I have to finish that sentence. "Technically."

Her body stiffens, but she doesn't run. She doesn't fold in on herself; she is still here, with me, but barely.

"It's technically not a mafia by definition. And I don't work for them, I run parts of the organization." While her body is still very reserved, her face displays more intrigue.

"While at Acadia, I was aware of the fraternity that everyone seemed to have a story about. How it was a cult, and that's why there were so many successful alumni or people, saying that they kidnapped and murdered people for fun."

"Gamma Theta Kappa," she whispers. It seems like even after twenty years, they still haven't fixed their reputation.

"Well, those rumors weren't far off. The Court uses that fraternity as an initiation ground for the children of Kings to earn their status."

"The Court?"

"Basically an underground society of the country's elite." She nods like I just said we were having eggs for breakfast.

"For the longest time, only those born into the society were allowed in, but when they started branching out, they needed help and created Knights, a group of men who have a skill or talent that can be used by The Court. We are people who have been recruited, not related by blood. We work alongside them, and even though we do a similar job, they are always above us in the hierarchy."

Her brows furrow.

"I had a few friends get initiated while in school. They tried to pull me in, but I wanted to go home and start my life with someone I thought I loved. So when everything went down, I made the call to Sebastian, who then got me in. They used my degree in finance to have me poised to take over this front company. I threw myself into work for them, and it paid off when they put me in charge of all the Knights."

"Why did you join?"

"Part of it was that I needed somewhere to go. I can try and say part of it was out of fear, knowing what I did about them. I could claim I was scared they would come after me. But it was more that I needed someone on my side. My fiancée had just cheated on me with my best friend, and my other best friend had known about it for years and never told me. My college friends were willing to have my back, and now the entire Court does."

"And I'm sure the money wasn't a negative, either." Aria starts to joke. That's a good sign. She is still with me and letting herself be comfortable.

"Yeah, that was also very enticing." I smile.

"So you're not the mafia, but are like the mafia? Does that mean you kill people?"

"Me personally, not usually. The Court? Yes."

"Not usually? So yes, just not often?"

"It has happened before. Everyone in The Court has it; it's a way for The Court to hold something over you, so you feel like you can't turn on them."

161

"Everyone?" She's not scared. She's curious. This is the point where I thought I would have lost her.

"Everyone."

"Wives?" That is not where I thought this was going.

"Most. Queens, yes. But the wives of Knights aren't as integrated into The Court. The ones who do become part of society do, but others don't, and aren't extended the same trust and privileges."

"Who?"

"What do you mean?"

"Like just random people? Like gang initiation?"

"No, we have standards." I laugh. "We don't just kidnap random people off the street."

"Sorry for wanting to clarify that the criminals had morals." Her sass is returning. This is the best-case scenario.

"What work did you have at Acadia?"

"When?"

"Right after you moved me here, that first weekend. You had said some of the young associates were proposing a project?"

"Right." I pause. How do I explain what happened? "A few of the guys who are in the process of becoming Knights got caught up in a human trafficking ring. "

"I'm sorry, what?"

"So we have these brothers in the process of becoming part of The Court. Their younger twin brothers' girlfriend ended up trafficked. They were able to locate her working a glory hole behind a laundry mat near campus. They wanted us to step in to retrieve her."

"Did you?"

"Yes."

"What happened to the glory hole now?"

"We run it now." Her eyes go wide. She's pissed.

"So now you're a human trafficking organization? Fuck all of this." She starts to get up. "Fuck you!"

"No, baby." I grab her arm. She tries to pull away, but I tighten my grip. I will not let her leave thinking I am exploiting women. "Listen to me."

Her eyes meet mine, full of anger, rightfully so. If she were ok with me actively hurting other women, she would not be the girl I am falling for.

"We own the laundry mat now, and still run the glory hole, but not with the women and girls they did. We took the girls out, set them up with housing and resources. The glory hole is now being serviced by the men who had kidnapped and trafficked all those victims."

I wait for her to fully process everything. Her eyes soften.

"You don't have any of the victims still working?"

"No."

"The ones working are the criminals?"

"Yes."

"Why?"

"Killing an entire organization would be too much of a hassle. We can't let these guys back into the public, they will just start over somewhere else. So now we can keep tabs on them, make some extra cash, and it is a kind of poetic justice."

"Killing them would be a mercy."

"A mercy we will not afford them."

Aria's body relaxes and lets me pull her back into me.

"Still trust me?"

"Yeah, I guess." She smiles up at me. I lean down and kiss her gently. This conversation could have gone so poorly, and it almost did. For a conversation with little to no preparation, I say it went well.

"Would you like to watch your show now?"

"Nope, you had said the twin brother's girlfriend." I nod. "Like the younger twin's girlfriend or the younger *twins'* girlfriend? Like are both twins dating this girl?"

Out of everything we discussed, this is what she wants to revisit?

"Both of the twins are dating the same girl."

"Interesting. How much information do you have on that?"

"How much information do I have on the love life of two nineteen-year-olds? None. They are literal children."

"I am only three years older than them," she says with the biggest smile.

Fuck, she's right.

"Ok, I'm turning your show on. I'm done with this conversation." I laugh as I press play on the remote. Let's focus on someone else's relationship drama.

CHAPTER
Twenty-One

ARIA

Last night was a lot. Between the anxiety attack and finding out that Theo is in fact part of the mob, I learned a metric shit ton. Unfortunately, now that I have had time to sleep on it, I have more questions.

I walk down to the kitchen and see Theo sitting, having his coffee on the island.

"Good morning." He puts his phone down to look at me.

"Morning."

"Hey, come here." He turns his body toward me, and as soon as I'm within reach, he pulls me into him. "What's wrong?"

"Can we talk about last night?"

"Of course." I sit on the barstool next to him. He keeps his hand on me, not wanting to lose contact.

"Your job." I fidget with my nails. "It puts me in danger? Does that mean I am in danger from The Court, or because of The Court?"

"Both. If you become a threat to The Court, they will do

what they need to keep themselves safe, but to The Court, you are an extension of me and will protect you the same way they protect me. If someone from a job ever wants to retaliate, it's possible they could try and go after you, but The Court will keep you safe." I nod. That is something I wanted to clarify, but it's not the question that has knots in my stomach. "I will do everything in my power to keep you safe."

I remain silent for a moment, not quite sure how to phrase this question. It's definitely not something I ever imagined having to ask anyone.

"Yesterday, when I left to make that call, I was calling Garret, making sure I had his promise to protect you. If you need more reassurance, I can get him on the phone." In seconds, his phone is in his hand, ready to call his boss.

"No, it's not that.'

"You had said everyone in the court has killed people, like it's some kind of requirement." He places his phone back down and focuses on me. "Does that mean eventually I—"

"That is not something we need to worry about right now."

"So, the answer is yes?"

"Possibly. I'm not sure. So much is changing within The Court right now that I don't know what is going to be necessary in the future when we get married." I just nod my head, trying not to get too excited about the *when* he just dropped. Not if, when.

"So what does that mean for my mom?"

"I don't know. She is getting close to saying too much about something she doesn't understand. The Court may want to step in. But once they do, they will handle it how they see fit." I nod my head, understanding what he's not saying. If The Court gets involved, they may kill her.

"Do I need to step in? If I do, what do I even say?"

"I mean, if you want to sit down with her, you can. Reiterate that you're an adult who can make her own decisions, that you are safe, remind her that just because you found love doesn't mean—"

"I'm sorry, what?" I cut him off. Did I just hear what I think I heard?

"What?"

"Did you just say I found love?" I have never seen this man blush, but right now his face is definitely a few shades redder than usual.

"I did." He swallows nervously. Butterflies swarm in my stomach. "So tell your mom that I love you and she needs to get over it."

"Ok, to recap, I am an adult who can make my own decisions, I am safe, and I am in love, then she might back off." He smiles, noting my use of *I*.

"I love you, Aria Mason." He pulls my body against his before his lips get firmly placed against mine.

I pull away briefly. "I love you, too, Theo Reeves." His smile turns almost feral as he picks me up and carries me to the bedroom.

CHAPTER
Twenty-Two

THEO

ONE WEEK LATER

"We still have time to call this off." This is the fourth time this afternoon I have caught Aria taking deep breaths and fidgeting with her jewelry. I can't tell if it's just nerves since the last time we saw her mom didn't go as great, or if she is just overwhelmed with everything happening this evening.

"No, we need to do this. If I don't at least attempt to help her, what kind of daughter am I?"

"One who was used as a scapegoat her entire life, having to live with the consequences of her mother's actions, and made to feel like it was all her fault. She hurt you. If anyone needs to try and repair what is broken, it should be her."

"She is still my mom."

"That's a bullshit reason. I have so much respect for you trying to make this right, but it's not your job to fix this. Your job is to protect yourself and find a safe place to heal from the decades' worth of harassment." I place my hands on both sides of her, pinning her to the counter.

My voice drops to a whisper. "You also aren't doing any of this alone, baby."

She takes a deep breath before turning around to face me.

"Thank you." I kiss the top of her head. Feeling her relax into me is one of the best feelings. Her feeling safe enough with me to let her guard down and willing to be vulnerable with me is one of the signs that I have earned her trust. I am so honored to be able to be this safe place for her.

Just as she was beginning to calm down, my phone rings.

"Mr. Reeves, Ms. Alana Mason is here. May I send her up?"

"Thank you, Enzo, please do. Have security escort her and have them remain by the door." Aria's body tenses as I say the words. I place my hand on hers and gently rub my thumb along hers, a reminder that she is not alone. I hope the second her mother gets here, Aria becomes the sassy, independent woman who won't take any shit, but in this moment, being able to be here at her most vulnerable and be let in to see her soft side has heat pooling in my chest. I don't want her to get beaten down and broken again by her mother. I would do anything to keep those thoughts and fears away, keeping her from hitting the point of an anxiety attack.

I knew from the beginning there was something special about Aria. Even in the brief conversation over drinks at the bar, I knew there was something different. Everything worked out perfectly for me to be able to be in this position with her. I will thank whatever force of the universe that brought us together until my dying breath.

As expected, a few moments later, there is a knock at the door.

I lead Aria to the table before I make my way to the front door. The moment I open the door, I am already regretting this idea. I want to hand her over to The Court, and this chapter just be finished, but Aria needs this conversation. The *what-ifs* would literally eat her alive if she didn't try to fix things.

"Alana."

"Theo."

"I would like to remind you that we have invited you into our home. If any behavior is out of line, we will have you escorted out." My warning goes unheard as she pushes past me and immediately tries to fawn over Aria, who wants none of it.

"Aria! Are you ok?" Her mock concern is almost believable. I want to step in and tell her to back off, but Aria handles it on her own.

"Don't touch me," Aria snaps, pulling her arm away.

"Let's all sit, "I offer, gesturing at the chairs. At least if we're all sitting, I can be between Aria and Alana, creating a buffer. I couldn't give two shits if Alana is comfortable, I just need to make sure I can get in between them if things become too much. They both move to their seats, sitting across from each other.

"I don't understand why we're pretending we're actually going to eat dinner like a happy little family." The mock concern is gone. "Aria, you need to come home."

"I am home." I cannot help but smile at the pure confidence in her voice when she says that.

Yes, baby, you are home.

"Fine, you need to come back to *my home*. I will not let this stand."

"This? You mean my relationship with Theo? Why do you think you get any say?"

"Do you understand what this relationship is doing to my life right now?"

"No, nor do I care. Considering this relationship is about me and Theo, the only people I care about it affecting are us." The strong woman that I know she has inside her has come out. She is not showing her mom any of the fear or hurt. She is standing on her own two feet, fighting a battle she should never have been involved in. *God, I love this woman.*

"Everyone knows you two are together!" Alana shouts. "I have to hear everyone talk about how I get to watch as my daughter dates the man I was supposed to marry! Everyone is talking about it!"

"We didn't tell them. Neither of us has posted on social media, so the only way they would have known is if you started bitching about it."

"I told a few people, knowing they would be on my side," she tries to explain.

"I'm sorry, what side is that? How do you have a side in my relationship?" Aria laughs, knowing somehow her mom has spun the narrative to be the victim.

"That my daughter is such a hateful, little bitch she started fucking my—"

My entire body tenses as I stand and interrupt.

"Alana, watch the way you talk to my girlfriend."

"Your girlfriend? Is that what you convinced her she is? And not just a pawn in your revenge?"

"Wait, which am I? A hateful little bitch or one of Theo's helpless victims? You can't have it both ways, Mom."

"It depends on how you decide to handle today. If you come back with me, we will just tell everyone that Theo manipulated you and used you. You didn't know what you were doing, and I saved you." My grip on the table tightens to the point I might actually break this table.

"Or if you stay, you will just be an ungrateful whore who fucked my sloppy seconds for a couple dollars. I mean, the entire town already thinks I fucked him for his money. I guess the apple doesn't fall far from the tree." Alana leans back in her chair with a smug smile. She thinks she won.

"And you think I care enough about what some strangers who have treated me like shit my entire life think about my relationship? That's where you're wrong. You may care what everyone thinks of you, but I don't. Because of your actions, I was judged my entire life. I no longer give two fucks, especially now that I have found a place where I am loved, cared for, and actually safe."

"You think you're safe here?" Alana laughs. "Theo is dangerous! After our last conversation, I did more digging into Theo's so-called "company"; it's all a front. He is in deep with some extremely dangerous people." How much more digging did she do? What did she find? This may no longer be a situation Aria has any control over.

"You said all this before, why would I believe you now?" Aria snaps back, doing a great job at hiding the fact that she knows exactly how much danger she is in and who I work with.

"Look!" Alana pulls a folder out of her bag, newspaper articles about a house fire near Acadia, some articles from the Acadia University newspaper claiming Gamma Theta

Kappa was a cult of the rich and powerful, another claiming that they were responsible for several of the suspicious deaths in the area, and another article alleging foul play in the disappearance of a local furniture driver. "These are all connected to Acadia and the mafia they have on campus!" Aria looks through them, and her mask starts to slip. Knowing I was involved with bad things is different than seeing articles about things the people I work with have actually done. This needs to end before it starts affecting Aria.

"Alana, this is all bullshit, and you know it. I think it's time you leave."

"So I am right! You hurt people! Aria, you're in danger!"

"Like you care. You didn't come in here and try to convince me to leave because you believed I wasn't safe. You came here trying to save your reputation." Aria throws the article clippings back down on the table. "Save the bullshit for someone who actually gives a fuck." Aria walks over to the bookshelf in the other room before returning with a handful of paperwork.

"Theo had these drawn up. You are no longer allowed to be within 1000 feet of me, my home, or my job, and it seems right now you are in breach of that." Aria picks up her phone and starts to dial three numbers.

"This isn't enforceable. I was never served! I know my rights!"

"You really think with all the big, scary people Theo is in bed with at his job that we couldn't forge documentation of it being served? You really think that a man who can, let's see— set the house of a billionaire on fire, while the man was still inside, or stage a suicide," Aria points out the articles that Alana had accused me of being a part of, "wouldn't forge a signature to protect the woman he loves?"

"Loves? Is that what he told you?" Aana laughs. "He said that to me, too."

Aria leans over the table, getting into her mother's face. "Yeah, we all make mistakes. His mistake was loving you, mine was not letting 'the mafia' take care of you when they offered."

Alana's face goes white.

"Get out. Or I will call the cops and have you arrested for violating the restraining order."

"I will go public with all of this! Unless Aria comes home with me now!"

Aria stands next to me, "If that's what you want to do, have fun. The mafia loves attention. I will be staying here."

She stands and begins to walk away. "I can't believe you would choose a man over your own mother."

"As far as I am concerned, I have no Mother. "

ARIA

The door closes, and immediately, I turn to Theo.

"Are those true?" I demand.

"Partially. Yes, he was inside his house when it was set on fire; he deserved it ."

"Why?"

"To start, there is suspicion that he killed a fellow King to take over his position on the council. He then hired a man to murder the only surviving family member of that friend so she would not be able to take her rightful seat on the council. She didn't like that very much, so she set his house on fire." I accept that answer. And honestly, good for her.

"And these articles?" I point to the ones from Acadia University. I remember seeing them or hearing about them, but I never took them too seriously. There was a flood of articles being released about Gamma Theta Kappa at the time, like they were poisoning the school's water, or they were aliens. This must have been lumped in with those when they released all the prank articles, so no one paid it much attention. Now that it's here, and I know what I know, that one is basically true. So what about the suspicious deaths?

"That one isn't true." He pauses. "That wasn't a suicide. He was attempting to stalk and rape a girl on campus. One of the Knights stepped in, and it got messy. They staged it as a suicide to stop any questions." Again, good for them. It seems like for every question I ask, he has a reason. He told me they don't just murder people off the street, that they have standards. I guess hurting women is a quick way to meet those standards.

I take a deep breath.

"Okay".

"Still trust me?" The last time he wanted to prove I could trust him, he blindfolded me and tied me to the bed.

"I think showing is better than telling when it comes to trust." I smile before grabbing Theo's hand and walking him back to our room.

I walk into the closet and pull out a few of his go tos. He stands in the doorway, watching me, paying attention to what I grab.

I grab a box off one of the shelves.

"Those were a hard no on your list," he states while trying to grab the box from me.

"I know, but things have changed." I smile, taking the box and placing it on the couch. I place myself in front of Theo and move my hair over my shoulder so he can unzip my dress. I slide it off and let it fall to the floor. Stepping out of my heels, I walk over to the nightstand, grabbing the blindfold and cuffs. I climb onto the bed and kneel at the end.

"Are you sure?" Theo asks again. The fact that he triple-checks even after I said it's ok is the reason I trust him. The way he is so careful not to push me further than agreed is why I am comfortable enough to give him full control.

"Yes, Daddy," I say sweetly. "If I change my mind, I know how to tell you."

He smiles as he unhooks my bra. He walks into the closet and finds my favorite set of nipple clamps and puts them on me. I inhale sharply at the immediate sting. Once they are on how he wants, he takes the cuffs from me and starts to secure my wrists. He leans in and kisses me. The moment he pulls away, he whispers, "On your stomach."

I do as I am told, lifting my arms above my head so he can secure them. I am left bent over the side of the bed. Theo pulls my underwear down my legs before putting my ankles in the restraints. I wiggle my ass as he tightens them, which earns me a good spanking.

Theo grabs the blindfold from my hands and asks again, "Are you sure?"

"Yes." He takes a deep breath and then places the blindfold on, covering my eyes.

I close my eyes and let the room go dark. I can still hear Theo walking around me. Not knowing when he will touch me or where his hands will go, or even if he's going to use his hands, has electricity pooling in my stomach.

"Aria." He slowly draws out my name before something is between my legs. It's cold, so I know it's not him. I can tell it's small. I have a few ideas of what it could be, but before I can piece it together, it slaps against the backs of my legs. My body jumps at the contact. It stings, but nowhere near the level it has been before. He is being gentle.

Cool hands grip where the riding crop made contact. Theo gently massages away the sting. His thumbs slide up my inner thigh, finding the way my body reacts when he is in full control. He coats one of his thumbs before sliding it a little higher. He presses gently at my entrance, but doesn't push in. I try to find any leverage to be able to feel any more, but I receive a smack on the ass and a laugh from Theo.

"So needy." He walks away, and I lose all contact with him. "Should I give you what you want?'

"Please, Daddy."

"Since you asked so nicely." He places a lubed plug against my ass. Slowly pressing it in, I stretch around it until it's sitting where he wants it.

I moan as I adjust to its size. The more I squirm, the more my nipple clamps start getting caught on the sheets, pulling a little each time. The slight sting is just adding to my pleasure.

I hear the snap of leather behind me. He snaps it again louder and closer to me. He does it a third time, close enough to me that I can feel the air being displaced. When I feel the smack against my ass, my entire body tenses, and I let out a muffled whine into the sheets before I realize that wasn't his belt. It was fur. I try to think back to the closet and what would have fur.

He had a two-sided paddle. He usually uses the leather side. My abs tense longing for what he hasn't delivered.

My body sinks into the bed.

"Not what you wanted?" Theo asks, I know he is pleased with himself.

Asshole.

"No, Daddy," I grumble.

"You wanted more?"

"Please, Daddy," I beg.

"I love it when you beg." A snap of leather strikes across both my ass cheeks. I jerk up and yelp. I smile as the sting settles to a dull throb. I wait for the next slap, but it doesn't come. Theo places himself behind me and slides himself inside me.

His hand runs up my back before sliding it up the back of my head. Gripping my hair, he pulls gently. My breath hitches as he begins to pulse in and out of me.

"Give me a color, baby." Something cold and sharp grazes my leg. He opened the box.

"Green. Neon green," I moan.

"So fucking perfect." He fucks me hard, but my focus is on the pinpoint sensation being run up my spine. It's slow, deliberate.

Theo pulls my head back, giving him access to my throat. I choke on air as the cold metal is placed against my neck.

He is fucking me while holding a knife to my throat, and somehow it's the hottest thing he has ever done to me.

"Cum with me, baby," he groans, and the moment he gives me permission, the tension coiling inside me snaps, and a wave of electricity floods my system. Theo groans as he buries himself deep inside me. The pulsing of his cock sends shockwaves into my core.

Theo gently pulls out of me, removing the knife from my body. He releases my ankles first, then takes the blindfold off before unhooking my wrists. He makes sure to inspect me for injuries. I climb onto the bed, and Theo lies beside me. His hand gently rubs up and down my back as we both catch our breath and let our bodies settle.

"Thank you," he whispers against the top of my head.

I pick my head up off his chest and search for his eyes. "For what?"

"For trusting me." At the beginning of our relationship, he had me fill out this worksheet, and on it, there were some things listed that scared the living shit out of me. Knife play was one of them. I hard vetoed that, and while Theo never tried to push it, I could tell he was disappointed. But the longer we were together and the more he checked in, and with everything we would try, it all became less scary. Having a knife held to my throat is still not something I would ever let anyone but Theo do. But he has earned my trust. He has made me feel safe. He has proven he will do whatever it takes to make me comfortable in the uncomfortable.

CHAPTER
Twenty~Four

THEO

TWO WEEKS LATER

"Reeves," I answer my phone.

"It's Maddox. We need you at Acadia, now." Garret's voice is different. Usually, when he is letting me know I am needed, it is more casual. Today, his tone is more somber, my clue that whatever is happening is serious.

"I'll set up a jet. Let me just call Aria and let her know—"

"Bring her; she needs to be a part of this." This catches me off guard. She isn't a member of The Court—yet. There are very few reasons she would need to be involved.

"Will do, wheels up in an hour." The call ends, and I immediately start sending the messages needed to have the plane ready to take off the second we get there.

"Yes, Mr. Reeves."

"We need to go pick up Aria, now."

"Yes, sir, I'll pull the car around."

I throw a couple days' worth of my clothes into a suitcase. I look at all of Aria's things and know I will not grab the right stuff. I don't think we will have to stay overnight, but I want to be prepared just in case.

"Mia, I need you at the penthouse now," I bark into my phone.

"Yes, sir. On my way."

"Let yourself in and then pack Aria for three days. We have a meeting at Acadia. This needs to be done quickly, and you need to meet us at the FTO in less than an hour."

"Yes, sir, no problem."

I meet Stan at the front of the building. He loads my suitcase, and I use the time on the drive to message Kai and let him know what is going on.

> On my way to pick up Aria.

> Again? You do know she has real work, right?

> And even with the disruptions, she has still outperformed every other intern you have. Not my choice, Maddox made the call.

> Done. I'll pull her from the meeting.

Stan pulls up to the front of the building, and I am out of the car before he has a chance to even put the car in park.

"Don't go anywhere, we will be right down."

I head inside and ignore the greeting offered to me, and head straight for the elevator that will get me upstairs the fastest.

I make it to Kai's office. He isn't here, which hopefully means he is already pulling Aria from whatever they have her doing.

I wait at her desk as she walks out of the conference room. She starts to ask Kai something, but I can't make out what he said. He just gestures toward me, and Aria follows.

"Theo, what's going on?"

"Pack up, we need to go."

"Where?"

"Acadia." My voice soft, so as not to let anyone who isn't supposed to know hear. She packs her laptop and pulls a stack of paperwork to slide into her portfolio.

"Why?"

"I wish I could tell you, but I can only speculate."

"What do I tell Kai? Or the team?"

"Kai knows, and everyone else will hear that you had a family emergency."

"Ok, I have everything. Are we stopping at home?"

"No, Mia is meeting us at the FTO with your bag. I don't think we will need it, but I like to be prepared."

"Ok. Let's go."

We make it downstairs, and I am trying to keep an eye on our surroundings. There are very few things that would require Aria to attend a meeting at Acadia. On the off chance we are meeting because there was a threat to her safety, I need to keep my eyes open.

I usher her into the car, making sure she doesn't hit her head, and I give one last look to our surroundings before entering the car myself.

"Theo, what's going on? You're scaring me."

"That's not my intention, I just don't have a lot of information, so I want to make sure I am not inadvertently putting you in harm's way."

"What information do you have?"

"Garret called an emergency meeting at Acadia and said you needed to be present." She continues to stare at me, waiting for more information. "There aren't a lot of scenarios that would require you to attend. One of the only things I can think of is if there is a threat to your safety."

"Anything else?" Her green eyes search mine for a more comforting explanation.

"The only thing I can think of is, if they think you're a threat to The Court."

Her eyes widen, realizing that option one was the more desirable option.

"But I-I didn't do anything, I barely know anything," she stammers.

I place her hand between mine and look her in the eyes. "I know, baby. Whatever happens today, I will protect you." She nods.

When we pull up on the tarmac next to the private jet, Mia is standing there waiting with a garment bag and suitcase. I definitely would have just thrown Aria's clothes into the suitcase; I am so glad I had her take care of it.

"Mr. Reeves, Aria." She smiles. I am glad they get along. Aria deserves to have some people on her side, and Mia is good people. "Aria, I packed you several choices. I wasn't told what activities you would be dressing for, so there is a little bit of everything. I also grabbed you a few chocolates and a couple cans of Dr. Pepper for your flight. I hope that was alright. I assumed they were in the kitchen for you, since Theo never ordered these until you."

"Thank you, Mia, you are amazing," Aria says, giving her

a hug. I take the garment bag and suitcase, and slide them to the stairway where the flight attendant puts them on board.

"Baby, we need to go," Aria says goodbye and then ascends the stairs. I follow behind.

The cabin entry door is closed, and moments later, we are ready for take-off.

CHAPTER
Twenty~Five

THEO

Garret had a car waiting for us when we landed. We were brought to the cathedral on campus. I assist Aria out of the car and place my hand on the small of her back, keeping her close while leading the way.

We enter the front doors into the atrium. The walls are lined with computers, most of which have someone working on them.

We walk to the front altar where Garret, Tatum, and Sara stand. As we approach, the entry doors open, and I look back to see Eddie, Parker, and Grayson all walking in. This has me starting to worry. Why would they bring in some of the newest Kings unless we were here to discuss a threat they would have to handle? My grip tightens on Aria. She looks at me, and I just nod. I want to comfort her and tell her it's all fine, but I can't lie to her.

Garret looks our way and smiles. That is a good sign; if he's smiling at Aria, he doesn't have plans to make her disappear.

"Welcome back to Acadia." Aria smiles as he comes over to greet us.

"It's good to see you again." Tatum walks over to meet us and shakes my hand. Sara is just behind him.

"You must be Aria. I'm Sara, Garret's fiancée." Aria returns the smile and accepts the hug. So far, everything is good. Garret and Sara may enjoy their job more than they should, but they don't play with their prey, at least not outside of the bunker. If they are being friendly, then it's probably safe to assume that Aria is not considered a threat.

"It's good to see you guys again, not at one a.m." She smiles, and then men laugh.

"Unfortunately, Theo is a pretty important guy around here, and when he's needed, he's needed immediately." Garret smiles.

Parker and Grayson step up and introduce themselves. I don't know much about Parker, but I have had a few run-ins with Grayson. He is a senior this year, and if all goes well, he will be getting his King status right before graduation. I'm surprised with the shit he pulled they are letting him stay.

Tatum interrupts the niceties and offers for us all to head to the conference room and begin the meeting. We all follow and file into the chairs around the table.

Garret addresses the group, "So we may have an issue." He looks to Aria before continuing. "Aria, while we are glad Theo finally brought you into the loop, we are having an issue with Court security now that you're here."

Wait, what has she done?

"It seems even though we knew you were endgame since you entered his penthouse, it took Theo a little longer." She smiles with the slightest shift in redness. "Unfortunately, your mother doesn't seem to like the two of you together like we do." Where is this going? She doesn't need her mother's blessing.

"She has stumbled upon some sensitive information about The Court while spying on you. She is making a lot of noise, and it needs to stop."

"The Court has extended Theos's status to you, but unfortunately, we cannot extend the same courtesy to your mother. You either need to get her under control, or The Court will step in to handle the issue."

"How am I supposed to do that?" Her voice doesn't waver. "I have tried. We had dinner with her two weeks ago. Instead of apologizing or stopping, she threatened to black-mail us. I don't know what else I can do." Aria recounts the attempted dinner we had planned.

"What exactly happened?" Sara asks. Aria turns to her and starts explaining how we invited her over, and she threw out some wild accusations, started throwing insults, and was awful towards her.

"Is this new behavior? Since Theo?" she asks.

"New behavior, no. Since Theo, yes."

Sara's entire body perks up, "So it's his fault, but not new? Do tell."

"Since he dumped her." Sara's smile widens, and she looks at Garret, who mimes *I didn't know*.

"When did that happen?"

"Twenty-two years ago." Aria smiles. These girls really do like talking about relationship drama; no wonder those reality dating shows are so popular.

"Garret?"

"I did not know, promise." He smiles. "This is all news to me, too."

"And how old are you?" Parker asks from beside us. Not him, too.

"Twenty-two. I graduated last year."

"I thought you looked familiar. Great speech, by the way."

"Thanks." Her smile widens.

"Hey, can we get back to why we are having an emergency meeting?" I try to change the topic.

"Sure," Sara says before returning her attention to Aria. "We will have to chat later." Aria smiles as she nods.

Everyone refocuses on Garret.

"Your mom is making a lot of noise; we don't want to deal with it. If you have already tried to get her to stop and it hasn't worked, it really only leaves us with a few options. We can try an intimidation tactic, scare her a little."

"That won't work," Aria interrupts. "She spins everything so she is the victim, so actually making her a victim will just lend her credibility, and she will just talk more."

"With that, we are down to one option. We need to eliminate the threat." No one reacts, not even Aria. She either has already figured this out and has come to terms with it, or she is hiding her true feelings about it.

"Aria, if you would like to be excused from the next part of the conversation, I can have an initiate take you somewhere else. You don't have to be here for the details," Tatum offers.

I am ready to walk her out of the room, but she replies, "No, it's fine."

"Are you sure, baby?" I whisper. "She is your mom."

"Like I said to her, I have no mom." She either has fully detached or she is hiding behind a mask. I won't make her leave; she gets to decide how involved she is in this.

"At any point if it becomes too much, you can leave," I reassure her.

"Parker, Grayson, you will be on acquisition." They nod. "We have been tracking her location, and she still seems to be in the city, which should make it easy."

Aris raises her hand slightly, and Garret nods at her. "How are you going to spin this for the people back home? They talk, and they know she is out here looking for me. This would be prime gossip; people are paying attention."

"And this is why you're here." Garret smiles. "Tatum, do you think you can hack her social media?"

"Easily."

"May I suggest getting one of the daughters of The Court on this job? You guys are great at the technical side of this, but having Tatum post as a forty-year-old woman will not be believable," Sara interjects. She is exactly what The Court needed.

"Do you have someone in mind?" Sara, Tatum, and Aria immediately look at Parker. They obviously know something I don't. Aria being in the know already has my chest flutter. I do not need to worry about her fitting into my life. There is no forcing; she has slid right in perfectly. My missing puzzle piece.

Parker smiles. "Addie isn't a daughter of The Court, but will be a Queen after graduation, and is pretty good with social media." The way he is discussing his girl just shows how proud of her he is.

"I mean, considering what her first video did, she is better than "pretty good"." Aria and Sara laugh and share a glance. She is definitely going to need to explain what is happening to me later.

"Perfect. Have her come in tonight after class, and we will get her up to date."

"Once Alana is at The Court, I will take over," Sara states, and no one questions it. "I have a soft spot for shitty parents."

"Will you need assistance?" Garret asks with a sly smile. He may be asking if she needs help, but knowing him, this is just foreplay. He will be in the room where it happens.

The two begin discussing supplies they would need, and Aria squeezes my hand.

"Are we still needed?" I cough, interrupting Sara and Garret. Whatever this planning session is, it should probably be done behind closed doors before clothes start coming off.

While I'm sure Eddie wouldn't mind, everyone else at the table doesn't have the same proclivities.

"No, if you need to head out, please do," Garret says, not taking his eyes off Sara.

I stand and assist Aria out of her chair. We walk out of the room and back through the atrium.

CHAPTER
Twenty-Six

ARIA

Theo opens the door to the black SUV and leads me inside. I slide across the black leather seat, looking back at the cathedral I have seen hundreds of times. This campus was my home for four years, and I am seeing it completely differently today. Theo gets in the car, sits next to me, and closes the door.

What I thought was an abandoned cathedral that frat parties are held in is actually a secret society headquarters. Some of the missing students had to have been killed there. I'm sure hundreds of people have died in there. I have now been part of a murder plot there. It's not rumors or gossip; I just sat in a meeting discussing how they were going to kill someone.

I take a deep breath, trying to push the tightness in my chest away. Alana has it coming. She has hurt so many people, and her quest for being in the spotlight is the only reason she is in the position she is in today. Whether I was at this meeting or not, the outcome would be the same. She has made herself a threat, and The Court eliminates threats.

The tightness in my chest turns to nausea the more I think about what just happened. Trying to shift my focus off the murder, I had just met several important people in Theo's life, and they seemed to like me. I think Sara and I could be really good friends, and it seems like she had a not-so-great parental figure in her life, so maybe we can bond over that. Garret also didn't seem as intimidating today, and seeing how he interacts with Sara, someone who loves that hard, can't be all that scary.

Having Parker and Grayson there was both unsettling and comforting. These are guys I've seen on campus. Everybody knows about Parker and Addie, for that matter; he is one of the most loved guys at Acadia. Grayson, on the other hand, is known but not necessarily as loved. There were lots of articles put out last year that painted him in a not-so-great light. Even though we weren't ever friends, it was nice seeing familiar faces and not being the youngest in the room. Even though Grayson is a year younger than me and doesn't officially have his status yet, everyone in the room treated him as an equal. They weren't talked down to or belittled, which gives me comfort that my age won't be a factor in how I am treated while with Theo.

As long as I am with Theo. If our relationship goes badly, I lose all of this. I am not a part of this society; I am only being allowed in right now because I am with Theo and am Alana's daughter. If Alana wasn't the target, I wouldn't be in this meeting at all. I cannot get too attached; these are strangers. Theo may never be able to take me to another Court function ever again, and I may never see these people again, no matter how much I want to. I can no longer fight the tightness in my chest. I need to stop, I have to focus on something else.

"Daddy." I need Theo to distract me.

"Yes, baby girl."

"Can I ask for something?" My voice hesitant. Theo has usually taken charge. The times I have initiated it have been by pushing his buttons and egging him on. I have never asked for soft.

"Of course." He turns his body towards me.

"I need a distraction," are really the only words I can form.

"Do you want me to be the distraction?" he clarifies.

"Yes, please." He pulls me from the seat, pulling me into his lap. The partition between the rows raises, so it becomes just us.

"What kind of distraction do you need, baby?"

"I need to focus on anything but the thoughts in my head." His hands slide under my dress and gently caress my legs.

"I can help with that." He smiles as he lifts one hand to my face and pulls me in for a kiss. His touch is tender and sweet. With how much we both love to play, I sometimes forget he still loves me outside of all of that. I grab his neck and pull him in more. I want to forget about the crazy parts of our life together and just be here, with him.

He lifts my dress over my head, leaving me in just my bra and panties. He smiles as his eyes roam my body.

"I heard green was your favorite color." My cheeks warm as he gently pushes my hair behind my shoulder.

"Whatever color you're in is my favorite color." I start unbuttoning his shirt, exposing his chest. I love the quiet moments when we are lying together, and I get to study his tattoos. I trace my finger over the chess piece on his chest. A knight. I smile, finally realizing the meaning behind it.

I lower my hand to his belt and begin to unbuckle. Removing this belt has become second nature. Moments later, his cock springs free.

Theo lifts my hips while pulling my underwear to the side. Gently, I'm lowered onto his cock.

It's uncomfortable at first, stretching around him, but it gradually dissipates.

He places his thumb against my clit and begins to rub slow circles. A gentle pressure begins to form in my stomach. He picks up the pace, and I start to crave the friction. I place one of my hands on Theo's shoulders and the other on the roof of the SUV as I begin to take his cock deep and slow, lifting myself until just the tip is left. Each thrust has heat pooling in my core. I lose my rhythm, but Theo buries himself deep into me, as I feel his pulsing cock.

"Theo," I pant.

"If you want to cum, baby, do it."

"Mmhmm," is all I can manage; tension in my core threatens to undo me.

"Ride me, baby, show me how my good girl takes my dick. Make us cum, baby," he coaxes.

Feeling his lips on my exposed skin makes it so I can't contain my moans anymore.

"God, Theo," I cry out.

"Such a beautiful noise," he whispers into my skin. His grip on my hips tightens as I pick up my pace.

"I'm going—I need," I gasp. My nails are digging into the ceiling. "I—"

"I know, baby. It's ok, let go." Theo thrusts his hip up hard, slamming himself into me. He does this a second time, and that is all I need. I cry out as the dam bursts open and I let my orgasm wash over me.

Theo pulls me to his chest and lets me rest on him as I catch my breath. I nuzzle my face into the side of his neck as his hand roams up and down my back.

"Good enough distraction?"

I smile and sigh. "Perfect distraction."

CHAPTER
Twenty~Seven

ARIA

I look at my watch. I am not one to usually count down until it's time to clock out, but Theo has plans for us tonight. He hasn't told me what they are, so I have been left in anticipation, and I really want to get home.

There is an executive meeting starting soon, and Mr. Castin just led a large group of men across the floor to the conference room. I keep trying to refocus on the research I am doing for this new client, but every movement around me keeps pulling my attention away.

My phone lights up.

Everything is ready for tonight.

Can't wait

I put my phone away, trying to refocus on the task at hand.

"Boyfriend texting you again?" Jonathan leans against the side of his desk, facing me.

"Yup." Great, he wants to chat. The first time he asked about Theo, it was because he was concerned, but I cannot forgive him for talking to the PI.

"You're still with him?"

"Yup." Maybe one-word replies would help get the point across.

I don't want to talk to you!

"Surprising. Aria, you can do so much better."

"Really? How so?" He's not getting the message, so I may need to make it clearer.

"I mean, what does he have that I don't?"

"So your issue isn't that he is older or dangerous, it's just that he is in the way of you dating me?" I ask, knowing what the answer is.

"I—" I cut him off before he could backpedal.

"So let's see, he makes your yearly salary every week. He has a penthouse in one of the most exclusive buildings in the city. His friends all run Fortune 500 companies."

"So it all has to do with money?" He smirks.

I smile. "Oh, and there is also the fact I don't have to teach him where the clit is."

Jonathan's eyes shift from me to someone standing behind me. *Fuck.* I look over my shoulder to see Mr. Castin leaning against the wall behind me, with his arms crossed.

"Mr. Castin—" *HR, here I come.*

"Ms. Mason." He nods in my direction before focusing on Jonathon.

"I would be careful what you say about Mr. Reeves. He will be attending the executive meeting today, and you wouldn't want to piss him off." I smile at the thought Theo will be in this building. Just the idea of being near him sends lightning through my core.

"I'm not scared of that old man," Jonathan retorts. He really isn't making himself look good in front of our boss, not like I have much room to talk.

"You really should be. But I personally would be more concerned about pissing off Ms. Mason." Both their eyes flick to me. "She seems the type that would sacrifice her own family if it meant protecting those she loves." Mr. Castin winks at me, and I smile back. He knows. I don't know how he knows, but he does.

"Now, if you don't mind, I need to head to a meeting. I look forward to seeing what things you have to discuss in our end-of-day meeting." Mr. Castin walks against the back wall to the executive meeting.

I swear he had already walked past with all of the board of execs. I must have been mistaken; it's not like he could be in two places at once.

CHAPTER
Twenty-Eight

ARIA

I try to refocus on my work. We only have an hour left before our meeting. Meaning. I have two hours before I can head home and find out what Theo has planned for us tonight.

"I still don't get it. I mean, money is nice, but I don't see the draw," Jonathon continues.

"What I don't understand is how you could go to a private investigator, make some outrageous accusations, and still think I care about anything you have to say," I snap. I can't do this with him anymore. He is not getting the hint. He is not listening to anybody around him, telling him to tread lightly. Maybe he needs it point-blank.

"What PI?" he asks.

"Don't try and bullshit me. I know a PI was poking around and asking my coworkers for information on my relationship. And I know you told him you thought I was being beat."

"I did not! Someone asked about you, and I said I don't

give out information about my coworkers. I wasn't going to just hand over personal information to a stranger. I may be jealous, but I am not stupid."

I look at him and, for some reason, I believe him. If he didn't talk to the PI, who did?

"Your friends wouldn't even speak up for you when they were concerned for your safety. You really do know how to pick shitty relationships, don't you?" Elle pipes up from her desk.

What the fuck?

"What are you talking about?" I ask. What does she have to do with any of this?

"The PI was poking around. Your mom was concerned that you were in an abusive relationship. Jonathon had refused to tell him anything, even though he specifically asked you on your first day here." She looks at Jonathan in disgust. "So when he asked me about the whirlwind relationship, I told him everything I know." I just stare at her. I cannot make my brain process what she is telling me. She spoke to the PI and made the wild accusations of me being abused? Why? What did she even say? We don't talk, we barely even look at each other, and we haven't even worked on any of the same projects. Half the time, I forget she even exists.

"So you told him I was being manipulated and abused on what grounds?" I snap. The anger finally floods through my body.

"You think we don't see the bruises you hide under your watch and bracelets?" I look down, I don't have any now, but when I did, I tried my best to cover them. I didn't want questions or assumptions. But that is exactly what I got. "Or the fact that you never wear your hair up because of the marks that show out the top of your shirt? How have you never worn anything less than tea length? You have been hiding bruises and scratches since the day you got here. Do not get me started about how on your first day, he came in here making demands, and when you said no, he got angry. I am sure the things he whispered in your ear weren't 'have a great time' or 'I hear the chicken is good'." No, those weren't what he said, but he never threatened me or did anything I didn't consent to or want. He has been so worried about taking advantage of me, but no one sees that side of him but me. All they see is the intimidating and domineering man. I can see why she thinks this, but it still doesn't give her any right to go to strangers and state this as fact.

"Elle, I don't usually bring my personal life to work. I am here to do a job, one I am damn good at. But because you made false accusations to the PI, I was actually put in danger." I stand, if she wants to say someone is intimidating, let it be me. "Because you told straight-up lies to a private investigator who was hired by my mother, I had to get a restraining order to stop her harassment."

"You got a restraining order put in place because your mom actually cared about you?" she scoffs.

I walk over and stand in front of her desk, and place both my hands on either side of her laptop. "Whatever make-believe abuse you have convinced yourself I am receiving is nothing compared to the trauma I went through growing up. I finally got away and was finally safe until you opened your mouth. You were *so worried* that a man you don't know said a mean word to me, you actually put my life in danger."

Elle stands, putting us eye to eye. "And I would do it again." My fist tightens against the table.

"Aria." Theo's voice catches my attention. Mr. Castin

and Theo are standing by my desk. *Great, something else to talk to HR about.*

I start walking back to my desk when Mr. Castin speaks, "Let's go talk in my office."

I walk into his office, expecting to be fired.

The door closes behind me before he asks, "What was all of that?"

I take a deep breath, but shouting at my boss won't help.

"I am not sure how much you have been made aware of, but by your comment earlier, I assume most of it." He looks at me, confused.

"You had said I seem like the type that would sacrifice my family to protect those I love." I look to Theo, who is leaning against the back wall, making sure I am not crossing any boundaries.

He nods, so I look back at Mr. Castin, who just mumbles, "Right, right."

"Well, a PI has been snooping around trying to make a case that Theo is manipulating and abusing me." He looks back at Theo for confirmation before looking back at me.

"I had assumed it was Johnathon who had spoken to him, but Elle piped up and said she was the one who told the PI that Theo was hurting me." Mr. Castin looks at Theo while sitting back against his desk.

"So I told her, I wasn't in any danger until she opened her mouth and fed the PI lies. Now, because of her actions, my mom has dug her heels in further, and is now threatening The Co-" I quickly shut my mouth and look to Theo, my eyes wide. I may have just fucked up.

"The Court," he finishes for me. Castin doesn't react at all, so this is not new information to him. My body relaxes.

"I understand why you got heated. But I need you to take

a step back. I'll talk to Theo, and we will figure out how to handle Elle."

"Shit, don't kill her," I say. She's a bitch who needs to learn to keep her mouth shut, but I don't want her dead. The men laugh, which puts me at ease.

Theo walks up behind me and places his hands on my shoulders before kissing the top of my head. "We're not going to kill her."

"Ok," I whisper, slightly embarrassed.

"We just need to keep an eye on her without tipping off her dad," Castin explains. Of course, I had to have an issue with the one coworker whose dad helped build the company we work for.

"Let us handle it, but go pack up your stuff, head home for the day, and cool off." I nod.

"I am sorry. I didn't mean to cause a scene."

"Just don't do it again. I would hate to not be able to hire my best intern because she has an attitude problem," Mr. Castin jokes.

"*Fuck*, does she have an attitude problem," Theo growls into my ear.

Mr. Castin has a knowing smile on his face when Theo walks me out to my desk.

CHAPTER
Twenty~Nine

ARIA

TWO WEEKS LATER

I am just about done curling my hair when Theo walks into the bathroom.

"Going to see me off to work?" I smile, putting the curling iron down on the counter.

Theo walks up behind me and wraps his hands around my waist.

"Stay home today," he says softly. Not a command, a request.

"I can't keep doing this," I say. I love that my boyfriend and boss are best friends, but I still have a job to do.

"Do you have anything important to do today where you have to be there?" I think, and I don't think I do. I have my laptop, the files I'm working on currently are all digital, and I don't have any presentations. There really is no reason I can't work from home today.

"No."

"Then stay home, please."

"Let me call Kai and see if that's ok." Calling my boss by his first name is so weird, but it was going to happen eventually, him and my boyfriend being close and all.

"Thank you." Theo kisses the top of my head before starting to walk out of the bathroom.

"Daddy?"

"Yes, baby?"

"I love you. "

"I love you, too." He smiles before walking out of the room.

Something about how he asked instead of commanded has my attention. I don't know why he is acting differently, but maybe being home with him today will bring me answers. I put my pajamas back on and bring my laptop out to the couch. Theo is in the kitchen washing glasses that I don't think we have ever used. I just leave him be. Once seated, I call Kai.

"Castin Construction—"

"Hey, it's Aria."

"Calling to see if you can stay home?"

"Yes?"

"Theo called an hour ago, you're good." He laughs.

"Do you and my boyfriend discuss my work schedule often?"

"I wouldn't say it's often; he just worries." I can hear the smile in his voice.

Theo really does try not to overstep, but when he is worried, he will do whatever he can to protect me. But what has he worried about today?

"So all the time?" I can't help but roll my eyes.

"Ok, whatever. He had a valid reason today." So he knows. Why am I the only one who doesn't know?

"Would you like to share that reason with the class?" I would love it if someone just told me what is going on. While Kai wouldn't say no if Theo asked him to let me stay home for "personal" reasons, that's never been considered valid. What is happening today?

"Nope. Theo asked me not to, and you know how convincing he can be." Oh, I do. "But we also aren't expecting you in for a while. So finish as many of the projects you're working on, and we will reassign whatever is left." Well, that's not fucking ominous.

"Why can't you tell me? Now I'm starting to get anxious."

"Just know we are doing this for you. We want the best for you. Plus, if you stay home, you can't start any more fights."

"I didn't start it," I complain.

"Doesn't matter, you and Elle need some space. Plus, the less you see the other interns, the less guilt you will feel for stealing their job at the end of the year."

"So I am going to be offered a job?" This is news. I know it's been assumed, but no one who actually has the power to give me the position has alluded to any decisions being made.

"Aria, you are doing the same job as some of our junior architects, if not more. You are outpacing all of the other interns and are still showing consistent growth from project to project. We would be stupid to let you go work for our competitors." Hearing the praise from my boss warms my heart. I do work hard at this job because I love it. To see that those around me see and appreciate the hard work is very gratifying.

"Plus, Theo would probably feed me to the fishes if I didn't."

"He is not part of the mafia!" I look up to see Theo watching me from the kitchen, an adoring smile on his face. He likes that I get along with his friends and coworkers.

"Aria, think about it."

"Ok, he's kinda like the mafia, but so are you!" He acts like he is an innocent bystander in all of this.

"That's beside the point."

We finally hang up the call, and I get started on my work. Theo joins me on the couch. We just co-exist for a little while, and everything just feels right.

CHAPTER
Thirty

THEO

I have been pacing the living room for the last hour. Aria knows something is up, but I still haven't given her any information. She finished her work by lunch, so we have just been relaxing in the house since.

I don't fully know how to explain what is happening, or even how she will react to knowing.

She needed to leave the meeting early, and she needed me to take control in the car. This entire situation has been incredibly hard on her.

Garret sent me messages last night letting me know the plan has been put in place. Parker and Grayson have started the process of essentially kidnapping Alana.

They were worried she would cause a scene, but I could have told them that the second they give her any positive attention, she will do whatever she needs to keep it. She ended up being the one to suggest going back to their hotel.

The last update I got was that Sara and Garett were with her. With them being the ones in control, they could be done in five minutes or five hours. Now I just wait until I get confirmation that the job is done. That is when I will have to break the news to Aria that her mother is dead.

Aria has said multiple times that Alana is not her mom, that she has no feelings toward everything that is happening, but I also know this is something that, even if she has no feelings toward Alana, having any part in ending a life can stick with people. Those of us in The Court had a large support network of people going through similar things when we were all made to take our first life. Aria doesn't really have any of that; she has me. I am going to be here and support her however she needs to grieve.

My phone rings.

"Reeves."

"Hey, just got word that they are done, and it's over," Eddie informs me. Part of me is relieved; this is all over. Aria is no longer able to be hurt by Alana. There will be no more attacks on our relationship.

"Thank you. "

"Anytime, man," Eddie responds. I note the lack of a certain pet name.

"No, Daddy today? Finally over it?"

"Oh, absolutely not, I will return to only calling you Daddy after you take care of your girl. No need to get you riled up before you go talk to her."

"That's actually really nice of you."

"Doing it for her, not you." I smile before the call ends.

Now to tell Aria. I can rip it off like a Band-Aid and tell her, or I can gently ease into it. Either way, the issue isn't necessarily how to tell her; it's how she is going to react. I just need to make sure I let her lead. Whatever support she needs, I will provide. Whether it's comfort food and snuggles or needing me to take over and distract her, I will do whatever she needs.

I make my way to the couch. Picking up her feet, I slide under them so her legs are across my lap. She pauses her show and looks at me. She knows something is up.

"I just got word from Eddie," I start. She is entirely focused on me. "Garret and Sara are done. Your mom is dead." I brace for the crying, the anger, the regret. I am ready.

She takes a deep breath and relaxes.

"Ok." She smiles.

I was *not* ready for that.

"Aria."

"Daddy."

"Are you ok?"

"Yeah, why wouldn't I be?" Now I am confused.

"Well, I did just inform you that your mom was dead."

"I was wondering when that was going to happen." I was not expecting this conversation to be so casual. I guess when she said she had no feelings on the matter, she meant it.

"What's going on in your head?"

"I guess I'm relieved it's over."

"What's over? The time with Garret and Sara?" I haven't told her much about their job, but I guess by their behavior, it was safe to assume that whatever happens in those rooms, they *really* enjoy.

"She can't hurt us anymore. It's over." I pull her in and kiss her forehead. "Kai said it before, I am the type who will sacrifice family to protect those I love." Me. She is ok with everything that just happened, because it was her way of protecting me.

My heart warms at how much she cares about me. I

cannot imagine loving anyone more than I love Aria right here in this moment.

"Is it wrong that I kind of want to celebrate?" Aria blushes.

"How would you like to do that?" I ask, willing to give her whatever she wants.

"It only feels right to pop some champagne."

"I'll grab some from the wine room."

"We did also just had some new toys delivered." Her playful smile tells me everything I need to know.

I may have lied earlier. I can't imagine loving her more than I do right *now*.

"I'll meet you there. You know what I like."

"Yes, Daddy." She gets up, and I smack her ass before she gets too far.

Once Aria is out of sight, I walk to the wine cooler. Once inside, I pull out my phone and send a text.

> Plan some vacation time for Aria.

Can this wait until the summer?

> No

That important?

I sent a single picture in response.

You got it, man.

CHAPTER
Thirty-One

THEO

THREE WEEKS LATER

"Welcome to Motor Yacht Mayet's Mate. I am Captain Travis, and this is your Chief Stew, Sammie. She will show you around."

Aria looks up to me and smiles. Ever since she watched that Bravo TV show, she has wanted to be on a yacht in the Med. We take the glasses of champagne offered to us and board the boat. The boat is newly renovated, and while it is gorgeous, I can't take my eyes off Aria. She takes it all in, amazed by all the little details. I don't think she has realized that we are not just on vacation. I thought having her fill out the preference sheet would have been a huge giveaway. While she has said she wanted to be on a yacht, the immediate planning of a trip could have been a huge red flag.

Aria has decided she would like to lie out on the sundeck as we leave the port. Whatever she wants, she will get. I offer to go order us drinks, and of course, she is requesting a Dr. Pepper. We are on a luxury yacht, and she wants her favorite soda. I lift her chin and place my lips against hers.

"I'll be right back."

"Thank you, Daddy." She has called me Daddy thousands of times since we met, and it still has heat pool in my chest.

I make my way inside to the bar where Sammie is standing. She looks to see if Aria followed me in.

"Is now a good time to discuss tomorrow's dinner?" she asks quietly. I look back towards where Aria is relaxing.

"Should be." I smile. I reach into my pocket and pull out a little black box. Sammie lights up.

"May I see?" I open the top showing a pear-cut diamond with two side stones and a diamond rope band. Sammie audibly gasps when she sees it. I did good. Well, I had Mia's help.

"Can you bring this out with dessert?" I ask, handing over the box.

"Absolutely. We were planning dinner at seven, and you will eat as the sun sets. Then dessert and then..." she looks around before whispering "*proposal* and fireworks just as it gets dark."

"Sounds great, I will have her ready." I look back over my shoulder, almost forgetting the cover story I used to come inside. "While I am in here, can I grab a Dr. Pepper and a Macallan on the rocks?"

"I'll bring them out to you," she replies.

"Can we also get some Ferrero Rochers? She put that on her list, correct?"

"She absolutely did."

"Thank you." I walk back out to Aria. I stand back, just taking it all in. I am about to propose to the woman I love.

"WE HAVE SET dinner up on the main deck, if you would like to take a seat." Sammie has been amazing today, keeping the secret while also spoiling the shit out of Aria. Sammie and the other stewardesses somehow convinced Aria "to play dress up" and do a fashion show with some dresses from some local designers, and made sure she wore a white dress to dinner. They were also able to secretly smuggle a photographer on board. This crew knows what they are doing.

I lead Aria to her seat, pulling out her chair like a gentleman. She knows when something is off, and even I can see I am acting off. This may not be as big a surprise as I was hoping, but it will still be perfect.

As planned, the sun sets as we are finishing dinner. Dessert is brought out, and there in the middle of her dessert plate, surrounded by flakes of edible gold, is the ring. Her ring.

"While we started our relationship with a bang," I laugh and Aria smiles, "I can't imagine anything more fitting for the two of us. From the instant connection to the slow build of trust, every moment with you has been perfect." I swallow hard. Aria is watching me with wide eyes while covering her mouth with both hands. "Thank you for trusting me even when everything inside you told you I would leave. Thank you for letting me show you, time and time again, that you are safe and loved. Thank you for giving me every part of you, from the sassy brat who likes to pick fights, to the soft and vulnerable side when you need comfort." I pick the ring up off her plate and hold it in front of me. "When I asked you for blind trust one last time, I promised I would never keep secrets again, and I hope you can forgive me for keeping this one." I stand from my seat and walk to the side of the table before getting down on one knee.

"Aria Mason, will you marry me?"

"Of course." She drops her hands from her face, revealing the most beautiful smile. I slide the ring onto her left hand as it trembles softly.

She stands and pulls me up off my knee into one of the purest kisses we have ever shared.

At that moment, fireworks are shot off the horizon, causing Aria to jump into my arms. Flashes of light come from behind us as I hold her tight while she realizes what's going on. Her arms relax onto my shoulders. My racing heartbeat finally begins to settle as she lets me hold her close and watch the firework show.

The Next Morning

It was bittersweet leaving the yacht. We had such a wonderful time getting away, but Aria is so excited to get home and show off her ring. She has made it clear she wants a long engagement. Not much will change when she walks down the aisle, so there is no reason to rush.

I love being able to give her reassurance that I am not going anywhere, and she doesn't feel like she has to take advantage of it before it is ripped away. We have come so far in the few months we have been together. I can't wait to see where this takes us a few years from now.

I look over at Aria asleep on the plane's couch. There is a

bedroom on this plane, but since I had some work to complete, she wanted to stay near me.

"We will be landing shortly. Can I get you anything before we start our descent?" the flight attendant asks as I close my laptop.

"I think we are good. Thank you." I carefully stand up and walk over to Aria. "Actually, I'm sorry. Can I get a can of Dr. Pepper with a bendy straw?" She smiles and nods before heading to the kitchen.

Kneeling down next to Aria, I whisper, "Hey, baby. We're going to be landing soon."

"Mhhmm."

"Let's get up. Is there anyone you want to call first?"

"You mean you haven't told anyone?" she asks, still half asleep.

"I still haven't told many people we were officially dating."

"And you're about to hard launch a fiancée." She smiles. She stretches her arm before fully sitting up. She looks around for the soda she had before falling asleep when the attendant returns with a new one. Her shoulders relax, and she smiles at me. She holds the cold can in her hands, wiping away the condensation.

"Thank you."

"Of course."

"I think it would only be right to call Eddie first."

"Not Kai?"

"Nope, I'm fairly certain you had to tell him something to give me a week off."

"Fair."

The flight lands, and we barely set foot on the tarmac when she has her phone out to FaceTime Eddie.

It rings a few times before Eddie finally answers. The screen is dark, and sounds of shuffling come from his end of the call.

"This better be important, I just left Eden for you."

"Who is Eden?" Aria asks. I smile. While she is far from innocent, sometimes she is still pretty naïve.

"Not a who, a where. Hi, Aria, What's up?"

"Are you wearing a leather harness?"

"Don't act scandalized, I have been in that guest room before." He smiles, and Aria blushes, but laughs.

"Well, I want to let you get back to Eden, but I wanted to show you what Theo did."

"Trading battle wounds, are we now?"

"Absolutely not," I growl. I don't need him to get any ideas. He might like to watch, but Aria is mine.

Aria laughs as she brings her left hand into frame. Her ring taking up a large portion of her hand.

"Oh shit!" Eddie shouts. "Congratulations!"

"Thank you! So I guess you're stuck with me now, too."

"Aria, I have liked you more than him since the moment I knew you existed. I will happily be stuck with you."

Aria laughs before shooing Eddie off the phone. The call ends, and she looks up at me, glowing.

"Daddy?"

"Yes, Baby?"

"Can you take me home?"

"Absolutely."

The End

Epilogue

ARIA

FIVE YEARS LATER

A loud thud hits the side of the couch, followed by the sound of crying.

I look over the edge to see a little blonde head of curls slumped over.

"Hey, come here." I offer, lifting her and bringing her to my lap.

"What happened? Did you get an owie?" Her little tear-filled blue eyes look up at me as she nods her head.

"Oh no! How can I make it better?"

"Kith." Her little lisp makes me smile as I gently place a kiss on the knee she is holding.

"Do you know what makes my owies feel better?" Lettie shakes her head, her curls bouncing wildly.

"Ice cream," I whisper, and immediately she perks up.

"Yeth!" she squeaks.

"Should we go tell Daddy we need ice cream?"

"Ith ceeem!"

Theo walks up behind me and lowers himself to whisper in my ear.

"I really don't like you referring to another man as *Daddy*," he growls.

"I am not going to refer to him as *Eddie* to his daughter." I laugh.

"Then I guess I will just have to continue punishing you every time you do." His warm breath against my neck has my core tightening. I think I could go for a punishment right about now.

"What is this I hear about ice cream?" Eddie walks into the living room, holding the sweetest little girl in the world.

"She got hurt, and dessert always makes me feel better when I get hurt. I thought she should have some to make her knee feel better." I smile.

He puts Lettie on the floor. "Go sit at the table, I need to tell Auntie Aria something before I grab you a bowl." His tone is so sweet. Watching him become a dad has been so cool to see. He turns to me, and his tone is not the nice, sweet version he used with his daughter. "How about we don't offer sugary treats at nine o'clock at night right before bedtime, unless you are going to get her to sleep? I'm on my own here, guys."

"I'll get her to bed. She loves Auntie put-downs." I laugh. The tension in his shoulders disappears. "When does my bestie come home?"

I start making my way to the kitchen to find the good ice cream at the back of Eddie's freezer.

"Her flight lands tomorrow afternoon."

"Ok, I will be here around 11:30 to pick up Lettie, and she can spend the night with me."

"Wait, you're bringing the toddler to our home?" Theo interjects.

"Is that a problem?" He goes to respond, but I cut him off before he gets a chance. "What is your favorite thing to do when I come home from a work trip you weren't able to attend?" I see the gears turning in his head. He stays quiet because he knows what he wants to say can't be said around my niece's precious ears.

"We don't have kids, so we get to play the way we want whenever we want. You can go one night without me in bed, so that our friends can have a child-free night."

"I like her, you should keep her," Eddie interjects as he steals my spoon full of ice cream.

"Well, he did marry me, so he is kind of stuck with me."

"You understand that you are choosing to tell me no."

"And that means when we drop Lettie back off with her lovely parents, it's your turn to play?"

"Yes,"

"And I welcome it." Theo grabs my waist and pulls me in.

"You're in trouble."

"Daddy, I am trouble."

Acknowledgments

I have so many people who made this book possible, but the person I want to thank first is you.

Call Him Daddy was supposed to be a standalone creative break. I honestly didnt expect to have more than a couple of page reads a month. I paused a project to just right something fun. Now, at the time of writing this, just over 20,000 of you have read about Aria and Theo.

This 84-page novella took off in a way I never thought possible. One of the most common comments I received in reviews and on my social media videos was "Where is the rest?".

So thank you for taking a chance on my story, thank you for loving Aria and Theo, and thank you for giving me a reason to spend more time with these characters. If it weren't for the readers of Call Him Daddy, there would be no Keep My Secrets.

Now, to the people who helped make this book possible.

BRIA

You better have known your ass was going to be on this page. Thank you for being an unwavering support and a sounding board, even when my ideas are off the wall. Most of all, thank you for being my friend. I cannot imagine where I would be in my career if you hadn't decided to start a booktok account. I appreciate you more than I will ever be able to share with you. You have not only changed the trajectory of my career, but you changed my life. Looking back at where we started, we are achieving way more than we set out to. I cannot wait to see what we can accomplish five or ten years from now.

KENNA

BROOOOOOOO. This book would not have been completed on time if you hadn't stepped in to help me. Thank you for body doubling, letting me sob on your shoulder, and always being up to share my fast food. Thank you for being a consistent, encouraging voice and challenging me to be a better writer.

NIKKI AND TABS

I know you have only been officially on my team for a short amount of time, but you both have been supporting me for so long. You loved and supported me when all I could give you was my gratitude. Thank you for sticking with me and choosing to join me on this adventure.

MY STREET TEAM

You are a huge reason why so many readers were able to find me. Your support has been nothing but amazing, and I really want to thank you for believing in me enough to spend some of your limited free time supporting my author journey.

ALINA

You will be thanked with every book I write. Without you, there would be no Aria and Theo, no Acadia University, no story. You encouraged me to start writing and to keep going when I got discouraged. You have been such an amazing cheerleader, even from way over there.

MY "AUTHOR CLIQUE"

I love you all and am forever appreciative of all your feedback and advice. Thank you for helping me find a community and allowing me to be my complete self. Thank you for loving my stories and letting me be a part of the creation of yours.

YOU

Thank you to every reader who took a risk on a new author and helped make her dreams a reality. There are so many books you could have chosen to read, and you picked mine. It may seem like a small thing, but every page read is something I will be forever grateful for.

Until next time, drink your water, be gentle with yourself, and fall in love with every new story.

Veni. Vidi. Amavi

About the Author

Katie A Perez is a dark and angsty romance author best known for her breakout novella, Call Him Daddy. Her stories are filled with strong women, powerful men, and the spice that carries them to their happily ever after.

When she is not bombarding her team with podcast-length voice notes of half-plots and scenes that will make them cry, she is most likely learning a new creative hobby, even though she has an entire closet of unfinished projects.

Also by Katie A Perez

Anastasia Duet

Call Him Daddy

Joyeux Novels

Meet Me On The Mountainside

Keep an eye out for

Make Me Believe In Magic

A Single Mom, Brother's Best Friend, Forced Proximity Holiday Novella

coming Winter 2025.

There are many easter eggs left in Keep My Secrets, hinting at whose story is next.

Who do you think it is?

www.ingramcontent.com/pod-product-compliance
Lightning Source LLC
Chambersburg PA
CBHW070815180626
46818CB00001B/275